The Company of Heaven

The

Iowa

Short

Fiction

Award

In honor of James O. Freedman

University

of Iowa Press

Iowa City

Marilène
Phipps-Kettlewell

The
Company
of Heaven

Stories from Haiti

University of Iowa Press, Iowa City 52242

Copyright © 2010 by Marilène Phipps-Kettlewell

www.uiowapress.org

Printed in the United States of America

The University of Iowa Press is a member of Green Press
Initiative and is committed to preserving natural resources.

Printed on acid-free paper

Library of Congress Cataloging-in-Publication Data
Phipps, Marilène, 1950–
The company of heaven: stories from Haiti / Marilène
Phipps-Kettlewell.
     p. cm.
"The Iowa Short Fiction Award in honor of James O. Freedman."
ISBN-13: 978-1-58729-921-6 (pbk.)
ISBN-10: 1-58729-921-6 (pbk.)
ISBN-13: 978-1-58729-950-6 (ebook)
ISBN-10: 1-58729-950-x (ebook)
1. Haiti—Fiction. I. Title.
PS3566.H558C66 2010
813'.54—dc22   20010007649

For Haiti

Contents

ACKNOWLEDGMENTS

The stories in this collection were first published in the following magazines: "Dame Marie" and "Marie-Ange's Ginen" in *Callaloo*; "The Chapel" in the *New Arcadia Review*; "Meat" in the *Crab Orchard Review*; "Down by the River" in *Transition* and listed in *Best American Short Stories 2001*; and "Marie-Ange's Ginen" in *Best American Short Stories 2003*.

The
Company
of Heaven

Prologue: Saint Bernadette at Night

My first recollections of story books come with the scents, sounds, and textures of Caribbean nights and with images of a little girl curled in bed over white sheets covering a small cotton mattress that retained her body shape impressed and deeply molded in it. She holds a thin, glossy, illustrated book about the life of Saint Bernadette. It is past her bedtime; the rest of the house is sunk in a darkness that floats like a diaphanous veil. The family is asleep, what is left of it. She is reading in a light halo coming from a burning candle stub she stole earlier in the kitchen and which she stuck right on her bedside table with three drops of melted wax, next to the old radio her grandmother gave her, all the while fearing she might set the run-down wooden house on fire, but rehearsing in her mind which favorite things of hers she'd quickly wrap in a bundle before rushing outside for safety in case this catastrophe did happen, because catastrophes are meant to happen in one's lifetime, otherwise why would the word for it exist and what would it mean that werewolves smile in the dark? Most nights in Haiti, the little girl heard sounds of cicadas, calls from frogs by the pool, dogs barking in the hills, and distant drums that did nothing to trouble the dream-filled sleep of the dog stretched at her feet, the black and white she-mutt with hanging tits which one day showed up at the gate and was only allowed to stay because the child pleaded for the dog. Fireflies sometimes illuminated a corner of the pink bedroom whose walls were increasingly marred by tunnels that termites dug beneath their surface. Fireflies were both miniature angels and the glowing eyes of the Virgin Mary on her, this little girl who, at times, temporarily interrupted her pleasure in reading for that of investigating the area where fireflies made luminous designs in the vaporous darkness she loved, to feel the brittle hurt and damage created by rodent-insects to the insides of her bedroom's walls, discover some new trails by pushing her fingertip in another softened spot of the wood surface, break it open into a fresh ragged gap, and marvel once more at the thousand delicate, minuscule, golden pine-tree granules that poured down at her bare feet like sand of an hourglass that spoke of a different time, a different life, the Time when Saints themselves walked the earth, when Spirits were visible, when the Virgin appeared to Bernadette and said, "I am the Immaculate Conception," and yes, the girl will forever be blessed, she will live in a time when there is still Belief worth striving for, Faith worth dying for, but mostly, Faith worth living for, because God does exist, the Word is among us, does care and watches over us, applauds what use we make of language, is amused by our struggle to express the inexpressible in us for which there are still no words.

Down
by the
River

It is Saturday, eleven in the morning, so Angelina sits and waits by the phone. Most Saturdays she sits in the big office chair that used to be my father's. I imagine her legs are stretched, her toes fan out in the hot October air. Her pigtails carry two barrettes each, one at the base and one at the tip, and she is wearing the white dress her uncle Noula bought her to wear at her father's funeral, back in May. The Saturday phone call is the big event of her week. Beginning each Wednesday, Maxènn, who volunteered to take care of her, tells Angelina that there are only three days to go. Friday evenings, while she settles on her mat to sleep, he tells her, It's tomorrow, and she always replies, I wish it were morning already!

On Saturday mornings, Angelina wakes up early. Maxènn and his daughters, who are seven and nine years old, get her ready. The girls came from the provinces to stay with their father during the summer months. A clean dress—one of four—is ironed. Angelina is bathed, soaped, shampooed, teased, tickled, dried, and dressed. Maxènn's daughters compete to oil and comb her hair. They love her. Angelina has begun to develop bald spots on her scalp, particularly on the right side, where the girls start the combing, their energy fresh, their attention focused. Hair is important to little girls, but nappy hair isn't easy; it takes more practice. When eleven o'clock draws near, Angelina is ready. The little girl takes Maxènn's hand, and together they climb the steep and narrow stairs that lead through the garden to the big house with the telephone.

Angelina's father, Sovè, died spitting blood, undiagnosed, the way people in the slums die—suffering from an unnamed ailment for months or years until the body gives out—and with more children already underground than jumping rope on the swept dirt in front of the one-room hut where sleeping mats are rolled up in a corner.

Sovè loved Angelina: everyone who knew him says so. Angelina had been only eighteen months old when her mother, Fifi, died. Fifi wasn't even sick; she just collapsed one afternoon, complaining of stomach pains. Her neighbors carried her to bed. For long, worried hours, Angelina watched her mother's friend Elmita fetch water from the nearby stream, then offer a sip to Fifi's trembling lips, sponging a face Angelina would never remember, a face without a photograph. That same evening, Fifi died. Sovè was still at work.

Fifi came from the northern town of Cap-Haitien. "On bèl moun bouch ròz"—A pretty girl with pink lips, that's what the neighbors said about her. "Li te renmen chante"—She liked to sing. No one ever saw Fifi's family. None of them came to her funeral. The last words she managed to utter before dying were to Elmita: "M kite ti pitit mwen nan men w, li va rele w Manman"—I leave my baby in your hands; she will call you Mother.

That is how Angelina came to think of Elmita as her mother. Most days, she went next door to Elmita's while Sovè crossed the river to work in my father's garden. Every night, he cooked rice and beans for dinner. Just rice and beans. And on some nights, nothing. Some nights she ate slum-dirt, though she says she was not allowed to. Sometimes he would bring her a mango from the garden. Sovè was a quiet man, and he liked to interpret dreams for people.

His brother Noula, on the other hand, makes up dreams, tells Bouki and Malice stories—tales of greed and trickery. And Noula drinks *kleren*. When he is drunk, noisy with songs, noisy in the head with noisy Spirits, he likes to dance on top of the high wall that runs along my father's garden, overlooking the slums on the opposite hill. If you ask Angelina about the white dress she is wearing today, she'll tell you Elmita bought it for her father's funeral, but actually, it's Noula who bought it.

"I didn't cry," she brags, remembering the day.

"And what did you see?"

"Anyen." Nothing.

Maybe she really saw nothing. Or maybe a girl of three and a half has no words to describe what she saw. Maybe "nothing" was a wish. Or maybe the coffin was too high for her to see inside. Maybe the coffin was too scary, and she didn't want anyone to pick her up to look inside. The man she knew had nothing to do with the body that had been carried out of the house. She knew her father was in the box that sat in the middle of the church, but no familiar voice came out of it, no familiar hand reached for hers. Maybe she sensed that what was in the box was only an image, made to burn the eyes and sear the mind.

Elmita had told her to sit. So she sat. And now, stretched stiff in a box, the Power who every day had told her what to do was no longer telling her anything. Death meant stillness, black suits, the glimmer of black tears on black faces. But death also meant her first pair of shoes, her first dress, and a pair of red panties that she borrowed from Elmita's daughter, Jenny. Death, for Angelina, was also the beginning of Things in her life. Things wanted. Things needed. A white dress that was the very first dress she owned— not borrowed, not shared, not a worn hand-me-down, and yet that eventually gets too small to wear. A white dress that gets folded up, not to be shared, and put in a drawer. A white dress that is taken out, in time, bringing back a feeling like a fire in her mind.

In my father's kitchen, boxes mushroomed out of every corner. The stove and the refrigerator suddenly seemed out of place. The mahogany kitchen table, which once occupied center stage, had been pushed against a wall. At one end, my father sat for breakfast, for lunch, for dinner, alone, served by Venant. He complained about her food, her torn dress, the trash that was never emptied, the ants that got in the *biscottes*, the silverware that disappeared. He complained about the noise the cooking pots made, the crows made, the street vendors made, the neighbors made, the neighbors' cars made, the motorcycles made. He complained that Venant complained too much: "Mon Dieu ce qu'elle peut babiller! Mais ce qu'elle peut babiller!" he would say to me in polished French. Venant was unimpressed. "Lamè, sispann babye, banm zorèy mwen!" he'd yell at her. Mother of God, stop complaining; give my ears a break! Yet it was Venant who picked him up off the floor when he fell out of bed, dragged him out of the shower when he had a dizzy spell, sat him on the bed, dried him off, got a clean shirt out of his closet, handed him his teeth.

It was Venant, in tears at my father's funeral, wearing a black dress, black shoes, black hat, dark glasses, standing in front of my father's corpse, scolding him, complaining that he should have known better than to get into that truck, known better than to get excited and scream at the workmen all morning under the sun without a proper hat. Hadn't she told him? Hadn't she told him? "Misye Emanyèl, èske m pa t di w?" Venant, arms raised to the sky, beating her chest, hitting her sides, invoking God, telling him it can't be that she is standing here, midday, before Misye Emanyèl lying in his coffin. Venant, ready to drop to the ground in protest. My mother, embarrassed, telling her to go and sit.

In the boxes were things my father had bought. Out of the boxes came Persian rugs, chandeliers, crystal vases, antique mirrors, Degas lithographs purchased in Paris, paintings of Haiti and French Provence and of black girls' breasts and white girls' rumps, bouquets of primroses, Tiffany lamps, porcelain dishes, crystal glasses, silverware, embroidered doilies, linen and lace tablecloths, sheets, towels, pillows, silver corkscrews, coat hangers, shoeshine sponges, batteries, lightbulbs, artificial birds. You'd think he was getting married! And he was—to the mountain in Thomassin where he was building a house. He was espousing the mountain, the view from the mountain over Port-au-Prince Bay. Espousing a new life, away from the downtown heat, the dirt, the dust, the poverty, the slums climbing hills like fungus, away from his own depression, away from beggars who show up at your gate and wait there for days on end, hoping to outlast all your efforts to ignore them, waiting until exasperation finally drives you to ask what they want, and whatever they answer, you put a few cents in their calloused hands, the way you might throw corn kernels at a chicken to send it pecking farther away.

My brother, Justin, who had never moved away from the family home, was helping me unpack the boxes in the kitchen with Michèl, a man who did odd jobs for our father. The house in Thomassin was two months from being finished when Father died: the apple orchard had been planted; the *rocaille* garden was finally blooming. My brother stood at the gate and saw it happen. He saw the yellow truck speeding down the alley, wondered why Father was driving so damn fast, saw the truck hit a post, Father's head hit the windshield. Father was still fighting for breath when his right hand was pulled from the brake, his body carried out of the truck. Now we were unpacking all that he had carefully packed, all the things that he had dreamed of unpacking to decorate his new house, his last abode in life.

"We need a strong man like Sovè to help us carry all that stuff to the depot," my brother said, out of the blue.

"Pouki w nonmen non Sovè?" Michèl responded at once. Why invoke Sovè's name?

"Why not?"

"Sovè mouri yè o swa." Sovè died last night.

I had only met Sovè a few days before. I no longer lived in Haiti and had come home for my father's funeral. Sovè came to speak to me after the burial. He asked if he could keep planting grass where my father had asked him to—he had not finished the job yet. I said, OK, let's discuss it later. Then I forgot about Sovè. But he came back. Waited through the morning. I still couldn't discuss it. Day after day he came back, until the day was right. I went down to the garden with him and he showed me the bald spots on the lawns. We argued about a price and I won.

And now Sovè too was dead. My brother told us of a dream Sovè had recounted after my father's funeral: Father had asked Sovè to plant a palm tree in the garden and reproached him for not doing it. In life, Sovè was not the kind of man to have taken a chance and ignore the dead—Misye Emanyèl was fearsome enough when he was alive—and surely Sovè had been careful of Grann Ayizan, the ancient Vodou Spirit, guardian of family, whose sacred tree is the palm.

My father lies in the darkness of his own grave, under the apricot tree by the river. That is where he wanted to be buried. You know, I said to my brother after he told us Sovè's dream, just yesterday I saw Sovè and he asked permission to plant grass around Father's grave. Now, that same day, he dies. It seemed then that everyone was dreaming of my father and I felt abandoned—I never saw him in my dreams.

But when I heard there was an orphaned little girl somewhere across the river, something stirred. I learnt that Sovè had meant to plant a palm tree in our garden. He had always done the planting for the family. This gardener's seed was now growing across the river and in my heart. I asked Michèl, "Ki jan ti fi a rele?"— What's the little girl's name?

_____

I found Angelina on the floor, in a faded, flowered dress that was too short, too tight, and torn. Her hair was disheveled, her legs and bare feet gray with dust. Yet this was not neglect. This was poverty, *lamizè*. Elmita, chin up, arms crossed, a yellow comb stuck in the uncombed half of her black nappy hair, moved in front of me, barring the children from my view: "Ki sa w vle?"— What do you want?

When Sovè died, Elmita took Angelina in. Jenny and her half sister Nadine became Angelina's sisters. They were sitting together in front of their hut-house this first time that I met Angelina. She looked pensive then, and when I came back a couple of weeks later, she looked pensive still. Some afternoons, I would send Onèl—my messenger boy—to ask Elmita if Angelina could come and visit with me. Elmita would send her with the red panties on—red to ward off the Dead.

"You see this dress, Angelina? No, not that one, the blue one here with ruffles and pink *rik-rak* ribbons. Yes? OK, I will buy it for you after we get back from the lab. Yes, there is going to be a needle again. Yes, *Ti Chou*, I'm sorry, I know it hurt the last time, but the doctor needs to check again. We need to make sure you don't get sick; Sovè would not want his little girl to get sick like him, and he is watching you, and he knows you are strong and brave, and he is proud of you. Do you like this blue dress? Yes, this will be the second blue dress I buy for you, blue like the sky. That's right, that's where your papa is."

"Wi"—yes. That was the first word Angelina said to me, the first time I heard her voice. *Wi!* She did want the little white papier-mâché bird I was offering her—white, with a red spot on the head. She held that bird all afternoon, wherever I drove her, wherever we sat, wherever we ate; she used one hand, never letting go of the bird in the other. A few days later, I asked her how the bird was doing. The bird had flown away. I told her to tell Elmita that I said the bird must fly back to Angelina. It did.

Every day Angelina watched for Onèl on the trail leading to Elmita's. But Onèl did not come every day. When he did come, he never had time to reach Elmita's before an excited Angelina burst out of nowhere, asking, "Se men menm ou vin chache?"—Is it me you've come to fetch?

Seeing all this, Elmita started to hurt.

The first blue dress came from the Baptist mission and became a measure of Elmita's feelings about me. After I had bought it from the mission shop, Angelina and I sat down in the cafeteria. Angelina was facing her very first hot dog. Across from us sat a family of Mennonites—father, pregnant mother, and eight blond children. They knew all about ketchup, milk shakes, French fries, and hot dogs.

I had spotted the dress right away. There was only one left on the racks; it was just Angelina's size. I stood her on the counter next to the cash register and asked her if she wanted to try it on. She smiled. Back in my room that afternoon, I turned the radio on the Vodou music station and Angelina danced on the bed.

Afterward, when I asked Onèl to go and see if Angelina could visit with me, Elmita sent her with the blue dress on. Then I bought sandals. So Elmita sent her with blue dress and sandals. Then, one day, it was the blue dress and a new pair of boots with matching socks. Wearing those boots, Angelina looked like a black marble angel anchored upright on the slick mosaic floor of our house. Next time, it was sandals and the white funeral dress. Then, the blue dress and the black funeral shoes. Eventually the blue dress disappeared, forever dirty. Then it was Angelina herself—either it was too late, or she was sleeping, or she was too tired, or no one was there to get her dressed.

That was when Uncle Noula, Noula-the-drunk, intervened.

True, Noula's place is the poorest and shabbiest in the slums. True, you have to wait for the morning, when he is sober, if you need to speak to him. And true, some people laugh at him. Yet with his shaven head, sullen coal-black face, and shiny red scarf tied around the waist, Noula is no joke. He does not like small talk, and his head is not often clear, and he stutters. So Noula doesn't waste words. He knows he'll hit his mark better if he keeps his sentences short.

Noula had been observing the changes in Angelina's daily routine. He saw that Onèl had been going up the path to Elmita's alone, and coming back down with Angelina. He said nothing. Neighbors questioned Onèl on his way, but Noula didn't say anything. He didn't have to—people gossiped. At first they laughed. Then they became resentful and no longer teased Onèl about his job. Then Noula came to see me.

"Ki entansyon w?" he asked. What are your plans?

I told him about Sovè and my father. He said, "Elmita is just jealous; don't worry about her. She wishes you were doing it for Jenny, for her own, but she is a young woman, she will have other children. They already don't eat every day and her man may leave her, or die, and what then? I have no work—I can't even help my own. Sovè had two other brothers, and I sent word he is dead but nobody came—no one has money. If Elmita gives you trouble, you let me know. I am the uncle, and what I say is law. She knows that."

And hearing this, I began hurting for Elmita. Poverty, not jealousy, was Elmita's only fault as a mother. What gave me the advantage over her was not how much I would love the child, but that I could afford her.

Then, one morning, Elmita saw Noula on the slum's dirt path, walking up to her place. She knew he was coming for Angelina. She knew he would bring her to my house. He had done it before. But today, she would not let him. She grabbed Angelina without a word and took to the hills with her. She carried her until they were out of sight, then put her down and pulled her by the arm. The hills were worn down to hard white sand that looked like bone; nothing grew there except low, thorny bushes. Angelina was shorter than the bushes, and these scratched her arms and legs when she stumbled and slipped. At the top of the hill they sat near a donkey, whose tail, wagging like a metronome, shooing away the flies, was the only thing in motion under the leaden, breathless heat of the midday sun. They sat without talking, without explanation. There was not enough air for words. Elmita was crying, but she could not feel her tears. They stayed there, together, for three hours, until she felt it must be safe to go back down. So Elmita gives the signal to go. That waiting, in the timeless heat, was their last moment together as mother and daughter.

But Noula was still there. He demanded all of Angelina's things from Elmita. Then he showed up at my house, with Angelina and a small plastic bag. "Everything is taken care of," he said. "I asked her to give me the child back. You want her? Just keep her."

The first thing I ever gave Angelina was a small white papier-mâché bird. Some men see their death coming. The last thing my father told me, over the phone, was that he had bought a large white bird, a statue. If only I could see it! A white embrace of open wings, beautiful on the rooftop of his house in the mountain. In the last photograph ever taken of my father, the white bird opens its wings behind his head.

She had left with one dog and now she was coming back home with fourteen, at least. After twenty years in Pétion-Ville, divorced from my father, my mother was coming back. Angelina,

Mother, and the fourteen dogs landed in my father's home. Each one of them excited, greedy for this new life. "M ap dòmi! M ap dòmi!" I'm sleeping over! Angelina kept repeating, jumping and dancing on the large bed I would share with her.

Angelina stood nose to nose with the dogs, outnumbered, protecting a peanut butter sandwich that could be snapped out of her hands or her mouth at any moment. My mother introduced the dogs to Angelina by name, showed her photos of her family in France—her mother at her piano, her father on his horse, her grandmother's house in Paris, her aunt Esther wearing a black dress and wide-brimmed hat with a plume, all so Angelina sees we are not dogs in this family; she explained that my grandfather was very rich and lived in a great manor house. My mother gave Angelina one of her self-portraits and told her to call her Vivi: "That's the nickname my father gave me, and I do not want to be called anything else. Not aunt, not grandmother, and not mother, either." But what Angelina saw, hanging on the wall above the family portraits, was the large crucifix.

"Ki moun sa a?" she asked. Who is that?

It was the rainy season in Haiti. When something crashed on the floor, it was either the wind that did it or one of the fourteen, or more, tails. I gave my mother a large bouquet of artificial flowers—irises, roses, mimosas—in a vase decorated with swallows, all of which I had found among my father's boxed things. That same night, the vase was shattered onto the green mosaic floor. My bedroom became the place where Angelina could escape the dogs, a place I shared only with her. The room pulsed with Vodou music, the magic of running water, a little girl snoring.

I cobbled together an altar in the living room, and the centerpiece was a wartime photograph of my father at twenty, wearing army shorts, standing next to his rifle. He fought with the French against Hitler. Troops from the Caribbean had been recruited in Martinique. They spent several weeks on the ship to France, and then they arrived at the time of the *débacle*—my father spent the war running from the Germans with his cavalry regiment, taking care of a horse. That black-and-white photograph was his favorite picture of himself. In front of the photo, there was a bouquet of papier-mâché doves in a green glass vase, his black dress shoes, his eyeglasses, a knife, seven silver basset hound figurines, a candle, and a red rose. Every day I dusted the shoes and remembered his feet. I had polished those shoes for his funeral, but then I found out they don't put shoes on corpses. When my mother asked if she could have one of the seven dog figurines, I dismantled the altar and gave the shoes to our night watchman.

The hearse, and my father's body, and his coffin, had arrived at the grave site before we got back from the funeral mass. But generations of servants—maids, cooks, gardeners, masons, carpenters—were there, people who couldn't afford to attend the mass. They waited for my father with their families, standing under the apricot tree, next to the river across from which stretched the slums where they lived. Sovè was there. In a hearse filled to the brim with flower wreaths, Misye Emanyèl was coming home after three days in the morgue.

Aramis was there. He had been a butler for my grandmother, a carpenter for my uncle, a gardener for my aunt; he had done odd jobs for my father. He had climbed mango trees for me. He looked tall, handsome as always, but bony—cancer was eroding his body, hidden under a blue suit and bow tie. He had come with his children and grandchildren. Boss Anòl was there, with his wife and son—he had made all the doors, tables, cabinets, and chairs in our family house. Dyedònn—my grandmother's spinster maid—was there, grayed and withered, her once enormous breasts now limp pouches that hovered meekly just above her waistline. Madan Sentayis was there, without Sentayis—he had made it to Miami on a boat, and he was sending money to her. Their three sons had brought sons of their own. They really all were there, Venant and Marie-Ange, Altagrace, Michèl, Wilsònn, Maxèn, Monklè, Ivnè. They were there to bury our dead. We were never there to bury theirs.

I thought of the women in particular, those who had been mothers to me in ways similar to how my mother and women of the family had been. How to count them—dead now or alive still, who, through repeated exchanges or chance encounters, had contributed to the person I had become? I knew I would not be Angelina's only mother. I realized how these women, in what I represent, emulate, believe in, and pass on, through me would also turn out to be Angelina's mothers.

The workers who had been building the house in the mountain were there as well. They had crossed the river from the slums. Digging up the grave, cementing its sides, that was their farewell work for Misye Emanyèl. Michèl, who had been a painter, a carpenter, a mason, a gardener, a night watchman with a black gun bouncing on his left hip, Michèl was there. He stood down in the hole, helped lower the coffin. A chain of men was formed to pass the wreaths from the hearse to Michèl, who arranged them over the coffin. After a while, someone yelled that the grave couldn't take any more flowers. "Ki sa w vle di?" What do you mean? Michèl yelled back from the bottom of the grave hole. "Send them down, I tell you! They are his flowers: send them down! *Chak grenn*! Every single one!" He pressed and shoved until all the wreaths were in. The coffin had disappeared under a fragrant coat of many colors. The priest started the benediction and prayer.

Time to close the grave. But first, before covering it all with earth, a solid slab of freshly poured concrete had to be made right over the coffin so the grave could not be later despoiled by grave robbers, thieves after bones and odd magic. The men who through the years had built things for my father and at the end worked in the mountain house were now mixing their last mortar for him, tying their last iron grid, to support the roofing that would cover the coffin. They were talking loud, joking loud, laughing loud, remembering loud, and imitating my father—his peremptory bearing, his inimical impatience, his verbal assaults.

A boulder had been dug out of the earth at the site of the grave, and once the grave was covered over the boulder was placed back on top of it. In a way, my father was now the boulder in the ground. It was the boulder that now felt the sun, standing on the earth where my father once stood, facing the apricot tree, telling me that he wanted to be buried there, on that very spot.

I bought three bottles of No More Tangles at the supermarket, on my cousin's advice. When Angelina first saw the shower turned on, she said, "Ooh! Tout la pli on sèl kote!"—All the rain, gathered in one place! Getting ready to go to the swimming pool, she put her panties on, and her plastic sandals, then grabbed a towel and a bar of soap. The slums where she was born, being by the river, are more bearable than the Port-au-Prince slums like Site Solèy—water, that's the difference. For Angelina, a body of water was a place to fill a bucket or a place to wash. The idea of playing in water took some getting used to.

My mother said I should cut Angelina's hair short and that I should only speak French to her, like she does, and not the Haitian Kreyòl Angelina speaks. One summer, when I was four, I went to visit my grandmother in France, and she took me to have my hair cut and then bleached back to the blond it used to be in my first couple of years—it was enough that I was an islander; I did not have to look the part as well. Besides, she was a blond, and blond girls were what she liked.

Angelina likes blondes, too. When she came in the bedroom one day and saw the pretty black *affranchie* doll—freed-slave doll—I had just bought for her, sitting on the dresser, she said, "Pou ki moun sa a?"—Who is that for? But when my cousin gave her a blond Barbie, she took it, and gave it a name: Ti Alika. She keeps it in the bedroom closet so my mother's dogs can't get at it. Angelina sits on her chair, and she and my French mother watch TV together.

———————

"M ap chonje manman m," Angelina said to me. I'll remember my mother.

"I know that," I said. "You should, and I'm happy about it. Elmita was a good mother to you. But, you see, I can't stay here anymore. I live in another place, and I have to go back there. I came because my father died, like yours did. I live in America. Do you want to come with me?"

"Wi."

"Will you go up in a plane with me?"

"Wi."

"But you know, I have to go alone first. Get papers ready, lots of papers. It'll take a while. Will you wait for me?"

"Wi."

"I promise I will come back to get you. I will call you on the phone every Saturday. Do you believe me?"

"Wi."

"Maxènn will take care of you here until I come and get you. My mother is too old, and she has too many dogs. But you can see each other every day. You and she live here in the same place. Do you understand?"

"Wi."

"Do you trust me?"

"Wi."

"When I come back, I'll bring gifts. What would you like?"

"Pen." Bread.

So now, anything that flies, Angelina says it's hers. Every UN helicopter, every U.S. Air Force jet, every airliner, every bird. Anything in the sky over Haiti these days is coming for her. It's hers.

This Saturday, sitting in my father's swivel chair at eleven o'clock, she feels happy. This week has been special: her passport photos are ready, and going to the psychologist for an evaluation was fun. "*Li fèm sote!* She had me jump, first on one foot, then on the other; she asked for my right hand; she asked for my left hand; she asked me to draw a person." Maxènn always waits with her. She loves him; she calls him Tonton—Uncle. She saves some candy for him when my mother gives her some. She told him that when she is on the plane, if it's a Saturday, she'll drop a mango on his head at eleven o'clock. Last week, when he came back from an errand, he found that she had mopped his room and dusted the shelf. "I am cleaning so you remember me when I am gone," she said, "but when I am in *Nou Yòk*, I'll be white, and my hair will bounce down my back like a horse's tail and you . . . *Wap rete menm jan.* You'll stay the same."

Life
Outside
My
Own

Inevitably, she fell. The drop from the southern side of the pool was a good two meters. Ingrid and I had always thought the narrow terrace around the water a perfect running track. Her basset hound, Valentino, liked the idea as well and raced alongside us, ears flapping, unconcerned that one of us might finally trip over him. Also, there was a row of *parésseux* that bordered the southern wall—these plants grew on tall, skinny stems displaying full brown and pink foliage right at the level of the poolside. We saw them as a real protective fence. And yet, there lay Ingrid, unconscious, two meters below from where I stood momentarily transfixed in disbelief before screaming for help.

We had been little girls in Eden. Barefoot in the garden, I

walked with trepidation and awe, aware of only two worlds: the one that hung above my head and the one underfoot.

Help came from Muriel's mother who was nearby, picking some basil for the lunch's chicken. Ingrid was lying on the dirt path right near the anthill we often approached with disquiet and, once, with murderous intent, armed as we were with a pot full of boiling water. We crouched a foot or so away from the hill with legs so far apart I saw that sometimes Ingrid didn't wear panties.

When Ingrid came to, her eyes seemed to fumble in need of a safe anchor for a climb back to consciousness. Muriel's mother sat her up and she looked like a cloth doll with a nosebleed. She cried.

The grimacing parting of her lips revealed a broken front tooth and pink saliva. Her green eyes were blurred in an expression of unutterable betrayal. Asked about the pain, she pointed only to the left side of her head. Yet, to me, she seemed to grieve far more loss than the bit of hair and the bit of blood that came out of the small cut above her ear.

The bells from the Dominican monastery down the street rang.

These were part of the sounds of the day at noontime, back then in our Port-au-Prince neighborhood called Turgeau. Ingrid was carried back to her house followed by Valentino, whose head hung low like Ingrid's mother's lower lip. I went back to my house across the street.

I have no other memory of Ingrid after this one. It is as if she had moved away and I never saw her again. It is as if every other image of her after that day has been washed away by that of her fall. Dissolved as I was into her sensations, trapped into the green smear of her eyes, into the unutterable depth of her unexplainable existence, I knew of love—I knew of beings outside my own, a whole street of beings outside my own, heads outside my own, a whole street of heads outside my own, all of life outside my own, and my own—unanchored, imprecise, undone.

Remembering Ingrid's fall still brings pain like the one I felt that day when I was seven. The whole endless sky sometimes seems to be gathered around and hang on one reduced, uncertain cloud.

When Ingrid's green eyes were blurred with tears, she seemed, with her finger, to be inexplicably pointing to an inexplicably small reason that could not justify the horror in her blurred green eyes.

I imagine she was grieving her innocence and the realization that life meant to lure her into a fall.

Childhood starts with the same sweet fondants of dawn, but events are contained within us from the start. They wait in line like pearls in my mother's necklace, and one small cut, one inadvertent snap, all lets loose in unavoidable succession.

I imagine she felt the pain of beauty crushed open only to expose garish substance, even if only in a small cut. She experienced how it is that one can be estranged in one's body. She then knew that there is a lie at the root of life: she had had a revelation, unutterable as revelations always are, and in a manner suited to a child's intuitive grasp. Feeling so vulnerable was like being soiled.

Death had given her a light kiss.

After Ingrid and her mother left, followed by Valentino, I might have chosen to head for the Immaculate Conception's grotto where I often went. I used to walk on the very edge of the sidewalk, putting one foot smack in front of the other, counting how many feet it would take to measure the distance between my house's gate and the Virgin's. I thought that when I grew up I should like to be a nun and wear a dress and veil like hers.

But I went home instead: who does a little girl look for when the fish bowl has crashed all over the floor? I looked for my mother.

I must have hoped she was having her hair braided—she might let me try and braid it for her—for there was calm to be found in this equal squaring of the scalp, parting the hair into equal portions of black strands, taking the head as the globe in one's hand—a world whose mapping one can control—dividing it, everything just so, each square giving out an equal length of smooth braid that reaches to the other braid in the square next to it, a design where all can be linked, bridged, and bonded one into the other, into the other, into the other, all around the head, calmly, all the way down the neck, until the whole round head has been tamed into a net that envelops it, embraces it into an inventive, efficacious lace that turns trouble into art.

She must have said no. She always did because I was only seven and couldn't parse things equally. She must have said no because

I don't remember ever braiding my mother's hair. And she might have been doing me a favor because I was only seven and I didn't need to suffer: I couldn't handle the weight of my mother's head in my seven-year-old hands.

So I went to my usual hiding place—the chicken coop—where no one in their right mind could imagine any child in her right mind would crawl into this community of frightened beings, sit in the middle of their excrement, pleased with the clutter, coy cackle, and raucous panic occurring in their scud-coated cocoon. Because this was not a rich world's chicken coop, this was a box, just a wire mesh cage all the way back, back in the farthest corner of the back garden, where chickens were held, like plants in a pot, fed and watered, until they were grown enough to lose their heads to our Sunday appetite, have their feathers plucked after one last headless flight down a blind path, down only a few feet away from where the severed head lay surrounded by a halo of its own blood.

Marie-Ange's
Ginen

My name is Marie-Ange Saint-Jacques and I got on that boat November third with my heart open and my eyes closed. My mother, Venant Saint-Jacques, also got on the boat. She too did this with an open heart since she got on that boat only because of me, but, unlike mine, her eyes were open—they had to, you see, because she had come to watch over me. So, that Sunday morning, she faced the ocean, dropped on her seventy-year-old knees, took the scarf off her head. It flapped softly like a flag in the early breeze before she could lay its white square flat on the gray sand of Balanye beach.

The others were startled when they saw her kneel, bare her head from its cotton-cloth protection, expose her white hair and the vulnerability of old age—offer it all, whatever its worth, whatever the cost, with such a simple gesture as that of pressing the white square into the sand, neatly and with both her bare hands as if to say: "This is all I have and take it—my head and all the images stored in it." I knew more than they did, so I did not have to be startled and imagine what she'd be thinking.

I knew her heart. What was going on in it at that moment would have sounded like "Take all that my head has kept safe all this while—take my father's smile when he last saw me, take my mother putting cushions on her old chair to make me comfortable near her, take the trees, the friends, the old folks, the luster of leaves at the rainy season, my ancestors' land, my whole life, here! I am going up that boat because I know you are hungry—death is always hungry. More, give more! So here I am to feed you with my body—you can bite it, chew it, maul it, disperse it, erase it and erase all that my body ever meant to me or to anyone else, just so you don't take Her standing behind me. Don't take her! Change your plans, don't take my baby, my daughter who sees no other way out of her misery than to sell that bit of land we had so she can pay our way onto this boat and jump into your mouth. Take my life and all the good I ever did and remember I served you well—this has real weight. Dismiss the bad—there is no power in the bad."

They were startled and scared because they could see that she had no hope. She had no hope and that is why she was going up that boat. No hope for the boat's fate, no hope for them, no hope for her daughter on that boat unless she came and bargained with death—traded herself.

They knew too that she could have lit a candle. She hadn't. She could have lit three, seven, nine, twenty-one candles! She hadn't. She could have deposited flowers on that scarf. She hadn't. She could have offered an egg, white flour, white rice, and even meat—chicken meat, goat meat, cow meat, any or all meat. She hadn't.

The simplicity of that white scarf bare of everything else besides itself was more powerful and frightening than if she had loaded it with gifts. These would have been palliatives. Straw men! They knew it. With the determination of complete abandon, she had reached for the double knot behind her head, untied it slowly as if she were thus undoing any resistance in her or any desire to live. She slid the scarf off her head as one exposes the ridiculous simplicity and flimsiness of the self, and laid it all down.

They waited for her to finish and she, the most hopeless, was the first one to get up the plank to the boat and lead the way to the journey at sea they had all paid so dearly to make.

Each one of us here had paid our fare with all we had left that we could call our own. In some ways, we had also paid with the whole of our lives and of our parents' lives before us because it took the slow unfolding of all these life stories in order for fate to have brought us to that point, that day, to go up that boat. What they saw my mother do was familiar. Disturbingly familiar— her desperate deal was understandable to their anxieties, to their cramping, empty stomachs, their restless sleep, their dying children, their dying lives. Everyone here had made the same desperate deal. But my mother had one less thing than anyone here had—hope for her own self. But the hope my mother had was that if all of us, the boat people of Balanye, if we were to be lost at sea and engulfed by the ocean, if fate had it in her plans that there'd only be one survivor, one survivor to make it alive to the land of promise—America—that it'd be me. No one smiled at what she was doing, no one smirked, and no one stepped on that scarf on their way up the boat. Each one skirted it carefully, paying it the kind of respect they wished death at least would give them, if life never did.

By the time we had all gotten into the boat, the tide had risen and reached for the scarf.

The same Chenèl I grew up with and who sat on the deck most of the first day said the scarf followed us for a long while, undulating like the water's surface until something below pulled it down abruptly. Chenèl said that, then, his heart sank with the scarf too—he didn't know if what he had just seen meant the bargain old Venant made was accepted or if it was a symbol of the coming fate of the people of Balanye, all of us as one.

I had never imagined that Chenèl had a heart that could sink. Chenèl's step was always light on the way and to the usual "Kouman w ye?" he'd answer, "Doing fine, after God." I could never have imagined I'd be on this kind of a boat with Chenèl who repeatedly said about himself, "I was born in Balanye; I'll die in Balanye."

I too was born and lived in Balanye most of my life. Except when I lived for a while in Port-au-Prince with my mother and Jo, her husband. She then worked as a cook so she could raise me and put me through school. I became an elementary school teacher. People in Balanye say that my luck in life eventually turned around because I did not follow the ancestral command and become a *saj fam*—a woman of wisdom—a midwife. My mother had been a midwife like her mother, her mother's mother, her grandmother's mother and all the way back to the days of the plantations when the women of my family were feared because they knew Spirits who gave them knowledge in dreams and assisted them in their work. Everyone in Balanye knew my mother and she, being what we call in Haiti a *pèsonaj*—an old person—knew them all too. Hell! She brought most of them into this world. They call her Grann Venant—the way we call great woman Spirits in Vodou—meaning she has knowledge passed straight down from Ginen—Guinea, the mythical Africa, the mystical place of origin, the dwelling place of Spirits, the one to which we must return, in death.

Tony was a *djaspora*—someone who had left Haiti and immigrated to America. He had been gone for ten years when he turned up in Balanye with enough money to build the kind of boat we call *kanntè*, and to sell passage to Miami on it. Ever since he was a kid, Tony was always on a hustle to strike some mysterious deal, and we knew that as soon as he got half a chance he'd be out of Balanye. One by one, he managed to send for his family—his father and his two brothers. All except for his baby half sister, Claudine. We had heard he got citizenship by marrying an American woman in Miami and that's how he got everybody their "green card." It was taking longer for Claudine.

That kanntè took shape in no time on the Balanye beach and it seemed just the right place for it to happen. This had been the playground for all our childhood games as far back as any one of us could remember. It was the site of our adolescent dreams and first loves. The beach had marked us—it was such a part of all the significant events of our lives that it seemed part of the very fabric of our cells. And we had marked it as well—with hopscotch, ball games, Mardi Gras festivities, community meetings, Sunday meetings, and private evening prayers muttered in the wind while one stood on its grainy stage. And the sea kept having to wash our markings, tide after tide—our countless footprints overlapping each other in all directions, witness to how busy we were doing nothing, how busy we are just staying alive. And for the tide to wash over as well, there was body waste, human and animal, and this because the beach was also the adult world thoroughfare—this one taking his cow to some grassy patch at the other end, that one with his goats, this one with her donkey loaded with cooking coal on her way to the market, that dog sniffing garbage pails from one beach hut to the next.

Tony had come back with all sorts of ideas and new language like "take it or leave it," "time is money," "no money, no deal." We were baffled and disturbed. The news went up and down the beach like bushfire. That was all everyone was now sleepless about. We had grown accustomed to a life of utter and hopeless destitution. We wore our resignation as a kind of badge justified and redeemed through the daily injunction of proverbial wisdom in which all that happens to us is attributed to God's will. Now, the surface wisdom had easily been blown off and replaced by a state of continuous agitation. Tony's kanntè had awakened our despair because he showed something we wanted and could perhaps grab. The new footprints on the beach overlapping each other in all directions were all of people who had the one and same thing in mind.

He wanted five hundred dollars a head and said the boat was going to take as many people as wanted to go in for what he boasted was a "direct flight."

"Just give me the money and your seat waits for you."

That's how he spoke. But we watched that boat go up and no one saw any seat being built. No bed either, and no bath, no toilet, no kitchen.

"Tony! Just how many days is it going to take for us to get to Miami?" we'd ask him.

"No time! No time at all!"

And we were satisfied with that answer because the timelessness of time was a familiar notion. Time did not take time when there was nothing for us to do. Our own lifetime had taken no time. So, OK, we'll be there in no time. But by the time the boat was ready most of us still had yet to find the money to buy this timeless passage. When we realized that we had so little time to gather a sum of money most of us could neither add nor count, we quickly understood the meaning of time. Tony had said it—"time is money." With that, he also taught us the power of words— words like "deadline" which he flung at us as if with a swing, a word with hooks that caught and pulled in our throats. Where does one go? Whom do you ask? What can I sell? Trade? Promise? Steal? Where? When? How? From whom? To whom do I pray? How far should I walk on my knees? Oh God! I'd rather die than not be on Tony's kanntè!

Tony's wallet was getting so full that three days before the date set to leave, he gave the money back to people who had their "seats waiting," saying, "The fare is now seven hundred." People went crazy. Since yelling at Tony didn't change anything they started yelling at each other and were once again wasting what had become a precious commodity: time. And then Claudine decided she was going to be on that boat—she was tired of waiting for papers that never arrived, tired of being here when her family was over there, tired of seeing the Balanye beach. It's on Miami Beach that she wanted to walk.

"Hey? Why not?" we said.

And everyone got distracted by the idea—direct flight! No time! No time! Why should she wait?!

"Hey, Tony! Why not let your sister go? She'll be with us— she'll be fine. We're all gonna walk on Miami Beach!"

It was Tony's turn to panic and we should have worried about that—why didn't Tony want Claudine on the kanntè? But we got distracted again when Tony announced the price was back to five hundred and that since there were too many requests for space on the boat anyway, there would be no room for Claudine. Besides, he added, this was a business deal and he could not afford to lose one space on a girl's whim—he had a family to feed, important commitments in Miami, life is expensive there, so he declared, "Claudine is not going!" And instead of worrying about Tony's shifting back and forth, we were just happy he decided we were all back on, including those who had only given him part of the money just to hold the seat until the rest could spring from God-knows-where.

We had all gathered silently on Saturday night. Only those taking the boat knew the date. Many faces turned out to be unfamiliar. Some of us came from as far as Fort-Royal. We had kept the departure date a secret so we could evade the police who obviously had seen that a kanntè was going up at Balanye—hard to hide such a big thing on a public beach—but until you are caught on the boat and ready to leave there isn't much they can do about it.

It wasn't until Sunday morning at five o'clock that we left the shore of Balanye beach. Either the police were asleep or they didn't think we would dare launch the boat once daylight started. And Claudine had gotten on. No one saw her walk up the plank, and yet there she was, down in the hold with us, sitting next to my mother, her bundle on her lap, wearing a pink dress and a grin. Tony was nowhere on the boat to be seen and Claudine said he didn't know she was on it.

There was wind in the sail from the onset but we thought it was good. First because the wind-swollen sail looked lovely against the light ultramarine of the sky, which we could see from the opening leading up and down the hold where we sat, crowded next to each other. And then we were grateful for the wind because it did not take long for the boat to run out of gas. It became obvious that just enough had been put into the boat to get us far enough into the middle of the ocean and let God take over, if he would.

Though we had grown up by the sea, none of us, besides Chenèl who was a fisherman, had ever been in the middle of it. We were taking turns to go onto the deck—first to relieve ourselves overboard, and then, when we ran out of gas, to evaluate the situation and argue about it as if we could do anything besides be thankful to the wind pushing us towards La Gonave island.

We were islanders but we had never seen a whole island all at once. La Gonave is part of every Haitian's memory, from the shore or from the mountains; it's always there in the distance. And seeing it from so close was a thrill—we could witness the miracle of it, this piece of earth, this bouquet like a gift emerging out of nowhere at sea. We came out of the hold and sat calmly on the deck in an orderly way, next to each other like schoolchildren at recess.

Though La Gonave seemed as familiar and comforting as an old parent who had come to embrace us, we were slowly becoming aware that, only halfway through the first day, we already were people lost at sea, that we had nothing to return to since we had bargained everything we could in order to pay the way, and that our destination might be unreachable even if it were to exist.

The voyage was indeed a passage, but one turning into an ordeal—a rite of passage. Those of us who had thought of bringing food were taking quick little snippets of it so as not to attract attention and jealousy. No one had thought of water. We were hungry and thirsty when the boat docked at Latanye Point but the island of La Gonave revealed itself to be a barren rock. Chenèl had started a collection to raise money to buy gas. We had enough for twenty gallons if there was any to be bought on that small island in the middle of the ocean and, as we could plainly see, the middle of nowhere.

Tuesday morning, we packed ourselves back into the hold and left Latanye Point. People at La Gonave had not been happy to see us turn up with the wind, literally, on Sunday night. We traded clothes for bread. For our thirst we kept wetting our mouths with seawater. The wind helped the motor push us out again as it had when we left Balanye.

It was clear there were too many of us for the boat's capacity. Were it not for the wind we might not even have gotten this far. I thought that in spite of our discomforts and misfortune the wind's will revealed God's own; this journey was meant to be. Yet I also felt we were like rats in a dark, humid, airless underground trap.

It quickly became hard to sit on the bare planks with nothing to lean on. Before long, we were all lying down, side by side, our backs chilled by the water that had already filtered in and was swishing around in accord with the boat's motion; chilled by our own sweat which could have been from the suffocating heat and airlessness but actually was from increasing terror; chilled by the realization we had been sold out by our very own, the people of Balanye—Tony and all the men involved in the building of the boat. Some or all of them would have known the boat had no gas, was too full, and couldn't take us anywhere but to the bottom of the ocean. I shivered while I remembered Tony's words that the trip would take "No time! No time at all!" So we took no food, no water, not even for the children who were, by then, in too much shock to even cry, including Anayiz's baby. There was silence among us because we were beyond questioning, beyond arguing, beyond speech. We were without chains, yet unable to rise. Rising would have only exposed our complete impotence.

I remembered what I had learnt of Haitians' history. I wondered if there might really be some kind of biological memory. What we were experiencing in Tony's kanntè was the same as when we had left Ginen—Africa! This was the way our ancestors had come to Haiti, to Balanye, although, this time, the choice was ours, and also the hope—to reach a promised land called Miami.

And there we are, so completely drenched we feel naked, so fearful we are mute, bound anew to each other in ways that had become more complex. We had always been burdened by an old, common Creole experience. It seemed that for us then, history was copying an old chapter. One that linked us to an African land by now so distant that its very name, Ginen, had become only an evocative word, a mythical realm for Spirits and for the dead.

I held on to the belief that God certainly could not aimlessly allow such coincidence to take place. His presence and eye on me throughout the journey was the blue rectangle that, during the day, was the hold's opening cut out of the sky. I would not close my eyes. I kept thinking—no, this is not just a meaningless trick of history, we are on a mission, us, black people. Shipped out, shipped off, we are the people who can take any boat. Rip us out of anywhere, dismantle us and drop us any place, in the worst conditions for life, the best for dispersion and disintegration, and we regroup. We reshape ourselves from the void of hell. We are the people who can live how no people should, suffer what no people can spell out, the sacrificial lambs never comfortable on earth. Home is not on earth: this is the meaning we bring. That is the mission.

By two o'clock in the afternoon we passed the Môle St. Nicolas. We had already run out of gas again and the motor had broken down. But wind was pushing us towards more wind. At dusk we fell into the accursed Wind Canal. We knew it because we felt it. The boat seemed made out of bone. It shook like a fleshless carcass. And also, at that moment, there was Grann Venant's song, a slow and soft lament: "Nan Ginen m te ye, se nan Ginen m prale"—I came from Ginen, I am going back to Ginen—"nan Ginen m te ye, se nan Ginen m prale . . ." And the baby started to cry.

Winds like the arms of a forest grab us as if to suck us out of the ocean's skin. But the ocean is hungry and wants us! Pull from above! Pull from below! The waves are a mad mother who grasps the boat like a child by the hair to slap him, and slap him, so that his eyes and face swell until he is blinded, his head gets spongy and rings, his teeth feel like abrasive grit shredding his lips. And yet she still slaps and slaps and slaps and, in the hold of that ship, we feel like the teeth in that child's mouth and we scream and scream.

Night falls onto our cries. We are tossed without end one against another with nothing firm to hold onto, bumping on heads, crashing on the hold's floor. Mothers grip tightly the light bodies of children to keep them from being hurled too high and too fast and yet they end up crushing them when they fall back on them with fuller weight after a blow. The winds have arms that don't let go, that howl at their extremities, and that will bleed all night for this catch if they have to. Chenèl of "doing fine after God" tries to tie himself to the mast like he wants to say, "I was born-baptized on that boat; I will die on that boat." He yells at us that we should shut our eyes and pray.

But there are two feet of water now in the hold and if someone falls and presses on anyone for too long he'd drown right here in the boat without having time to think "Jesus, Marie . . ." A man jumps up with a howl, climbs out of the hold mumbling repeatedly, "Get out of the way, I am going home, get out of the way, I am going home, get out of . . ." A kick in the chest from Chenèl on the deck throws him right back down. Two men wrap their arms around him to keep him from getting up and out again; someone from a corner of the hold yells, "Let him go! Throw him out in the ocean! Too many of us in here anyway!" Others echo him from everywhere in the hold, "Throw him out! Throw him out! Too many! Too many!"

The man now screams, "Lage m! Lage m! Lage m, bagay dyab andedan!"—Let go of me! The devil is in here!

A beam of light suddenly shoots in the hold—it's Chenèl with a flashlight. He spotlights faces here and there. Then he aims the beam up the mast and sail. The light distracts us and stops the growing frenzy against the man. Chenèl's light is searching for something and finds it: a man on the deck stands briefly at the very edge of the black waters, arms wide open, his body an image of the cross, Bible in hand, face lifted to the sky, and, soundlessly, jumps. Suddenly, "Grennen! Grennen! Grennen!"—Scatter! Scatter! Scatter!—we hear from all over the hold.

It was pitch black. Who was saying it? How many? To whom? What does it mean? However brave anyone might have still felt, hearing this, one could only shiver. The word has an urgency, a heartlessness, a madness about it—my body goes limp with fear. And again, repeatedly, "Grennen! Grennen!" Then, right after, "Fèmen je w!"—Shut your eyes! Shut your eyes! Something terrible is here! Something odious is happening! I already could not see anything, but closing my eyes I felt so completely vulnerable it was unbearable. At this very moment, Grann Venant squeezed my arms and ordered me as well, "Shut your eyes!" I did, and just then felt the light going across my face—someone was flashing us. Voices were screaming, "Anmwe! Anmwe! Lage m!"—Help! Help! Let go of me! Let go of me!

"Mother! What's happening?" I asked with anguish and my eyes still shut.

"Bagay zonbi nan batiman an! Fèmen je w!"—Zombies at work on the boat! Shut your eyes!

Her voice was calming. I felt calmed that she seemed able to think through all of this, even though I didn't know why she ordered me to shut my eyes or what it meant that she kept hers open. But even at my age, I still obeyed my mother. Young people owe respect to the wisdom of the old. People close to me overheard what she said and started screaming in a panic, repeating her words, "Zombies at work on the boat! Zombies at work on the boat!" Suddenly I felt a lot of violent motion around me. Then, hands were pulling at me. But two strong arms held me fast while I heard my mother lashing out: "My child's not going! My child's not going!" Almost right after hearing her, it seemed that every hand that had gripped and pulled at my body relaxed and let go. I kept hearing "Grennen! Grennen!" until my heart could no longer take all the pounding in my chest and I passed out.

When I came to, it still felt dark around me but the boat was no longer being slapped by waves and there was no sound of water splashing in with every slap. My mother had told me to keep my eyes closed and I did until I sensed daybreak. When I opened them I saw that she was not there. Where was she? Where could she have gone? We were all in too much shock to make sense of the night and of all that we had heard and suffered. I thought this must have been a passage underwater.

I used to hear stories about journeys underwater made by the dead but sometimes by the living. These come back transformed by secret knowledge that can heal, give wisdom, attract wealth, challenge the world's sense of reality. The old folks said that the underwater world is a reverse reflection of the one above—that there are trees, houses, everything as we know it on earth. How, then, do we tell which one we are in and if we have crossed over? Was my mother gone? Or was I? Which one is under? Which one is above? The mast was broken and the sail was ripped. No matter what amount of wind would lift, the boat could not be led forward. People started to worry that we were going to die if the boat could not go forward anymore. But were we dead already? Were this broken mast and torn sail an underworld metaphor for the full sails of the living?

I sat on the deck with the others, amorphous, washed of feelings, and with these thoughts in my mind until I saw it: the island! Gleaming in the dawn, and with mist surrounding it that made it seem to float in the sky. There was no more division between blue water and blue sky. Morning mist smudged all boundaries and the island seemed elevated and weightless. We were too worn out to cheer but some felt hope filling up their chest again as if a gentle breeze had entered them. Claudine thought it was Miami. Chenèl thought it was Cuba. Was it either one? Or was it maybe . . . Ginen? Now, can you tell me? Is it? Is it Ginen? Is my mother here?

Dogs

Wednesday morning, an elephant walked the streets of Port-au-Prince after a visit with the president. The elephant was led by a dandy dwarf. This fellow had a large, red, heavily made-up smile on his clown's face, which nevertheless looked grim under a green top hat. There were two camels walking along as well, and four tigers kept two by two in a cage. On each camel sat a woman wearing a night-blue sequin dance suit, black-netting tights, and inch-long black eyelashes. The crowd that followed them, eyes popping and jaws dropping, did much to increase the annoyance, boredom, and heat discomfort of the tigers which leaned heavily against their cages' iron bars.

The crowd had never seen the likes of these creatures. People elbowed each other to get closer and closer—closer to see the tigers panting, the women smoking in sexy poses, the camels drooling, the dwarf cracking his whip, the elephant dropping dung on the newly repaved avenue of the Champ de Mars plaza.

The animals—from a Mexican circus in town for a couple of days—had just come out of the palace's gardens where the president had given a party for children. Like most of them do, I too liked the circus when I was a child. Now I don't.

But Vivi does. She—the one who prefers that I do not call her "Mother"—has created her own sort of circus.

She has Titus and Brutus and Melodie and Somalie. And she also has Jolie and Venus and Darling and Harmonie. While Katia, Noisette, and Puce are the ever-lounging girls, Sophie, Papito, Barry, and Max are her daytime gatekeepers. Nino is the only male allowed on the bed during the day. All of them are dogs.

They are offshoots of the gutter, the neighboring slums, or born out of her failed attempts to spay the females. Puppies live in baskets hidden at the bottom of closets or locked in the bathroom behind pulled curtains as if Vivi were growing marijuana. Keeping puppies out of sight is partly the way she manages space and partly done for my benefit.

At Vivi's house, there is a stock group of dogs I recognize each time I visit even though the whole lot of them are usually sectioned off in various rooms according to natural compatibility. And there are a shifting number of dogs in transit, those recently rescued, for whom she still actively looks for a home other than hers.

When I come visit, as I do today, I wear pants.

I find the familiar horde at the second-floor wrought iron door screeching with excitement or growling, baring teeth, depending on the dog.

Vivi comes hurriedly and orders, "Back! Back!" and, smiling, "How are you, Love?"

If they don't obey, which is always the case, she grabs tail, neck, skin, ear, whatever is handy.

"Wait, I'll get the keys."

But first, she drags one barking dog at a time back up the stairs to the third floor's partitioned area of the living room, after having been careful not to stumble over them while they resist arrest.

I can guess when there is a new dog because Vivi then displays ill-wrapped purple bandages (stained from methylene blue) around her toes, forearms, and fingers that get in the way of her sorting out the many keys to the many locks and padlocks of the many doors, closets, and cabinets of her house.

"If at sixteen I could swim across the Seine in the dead of winter, it's not a dogfight that's going to scare me."

But today, she is in her late seventies and age has taught her to fear what she reads in me. "I know why you are here," she warns me while she is opening the door. "I don't want to hear about it."

She locks the door behind me and we go up the tall narrow stairway that leads directly to the living room and adjoining kitchen area. The two rooms make up one large space. The steps look freshly mopped and neat even though there are some missing mosaics here and there.

Vivi suddenly trips. She catches herself quickly by holding onto the sidewalls of the stairway.

I regularly send someone to replace the missing mosaics that keep lifting up, not only so it looks better but mostly because I worry that the uneven surface of some of the steps will eventually cause Vivi to lose balance and fall. God forbid she might even roll all the way down the stairs and greatly hurt herself.

The cause of this constant state of disrepair of the mosaic steps is that the dogs never allow the required time for the fresh glue to dry before Vivi has to mop again—they relieve themselves wherever and whenever they wish, and the stairway seems to them an ideal, private place to do that. With detergent water seeping through the joints between mosaics and down under, the glue has no chance to dry and hold properly.

After nearly falling, Vivi elects to lift and hold the sides of her long green robe before continuing up the stairs.

I notice that her legs and feet are bandaged but so loosely that some of the bandage drags and I think they must inconvenience her being able to move properly. Furthermore, when she tripped a few seconds ago and held her balance with her arms up on the walls, her long sleeves were pulled and revealed that her right arm and hand were bandaged as well, while on her left hand she is wearing five of her favorite big silver rings, one on each finger.

As she finally reaches the top of the stairs, she takes a deep, satisfied breath. She turns to me standing behind her and smiles, her lips expertly outlined in Carnival Berry.

"Here we are," she says and turns left to head for the bedroom. "Follow me and watch where you step."

To the right of the stairs is the open living room. It's been a while since Vivi had every piece of furniture removed from there; she found it easier to keep clean, fewer things to worry about. But her walls, top to bottom, are covered with her paintings, black and white or colorful oil portraits of sexy yet anguished young women wearing long hair, bangles, and heavy mascara.

But lately, she has started to paint moon-filled landscapes where a long, tree-lined alleyway leads to a distant, half-hidden, mysterious manor house. "It's my dream-house."

As we turn left of the stairs, the kitchen comes in full view.

Today, the stove is missing and in the space it occupied the pink walls are charred and black from recent fire and smoke. The wood cabinet above where the stove used to be is burnt beyond repair and its glass doors are scattered in pieces all over the floor.

On the kitchen counter to the right, I notice among the pile of otherwise unopened mail the Court Summation envelope that came a couple of days ago as a result of the neighbors' complaints. It had been handed to me first so I could give it to her.

"How will you do the cooking now?" I ask.

"I have a little camper's stove."

"Shouldn't I get you another stove?"

"We'll see."

After passing by a row of empty dog-food dishes lined against the wall—plates, old cooking pots, yellow and green plastic kitchen bowls—we come to the door at the foot of which a partly bandaged dog lies on an old couch cushion, which its tail whips noisily from the joy of seeing me.

"How about food for the dogs?" I ask.

"Wilson came over. He'll cook outside. He'll use coal."

"Does your hand hurt?"

"No. I control my hand. It does not control me."

Vivi holds court in her bedroom. Within its walls, a group of dogs is granted an audience. All other rooms are time stations in which the rest wait for their turn. The TV goes on all day and she maintains a constant level of agitation throughout the house while she pampers the dogs.

Green lizards keep an undulating surveillance of her bedroom's ceiling.

"They are a family," she says about the lizards. "There are seven of them now. They like TV. I swear."

God forbid if I ever need to use her bathroom—she rushes in there after telling me she has to do some cleaning, then she locks the door. I hear big water pouring into a metal bucket. I hear small water and assume it's detergent. I hear her shuffling, knocking things, opening and shutting the closet doors until she reappears, shining under a light sweat.

"It's good now but hurry up. Call if you need anything. Don't open the closet."

If any dog resembles its master, in this circus, it is Jolie. She has developed into a caricature of Vivi. She plays the ringmaster in a manner similar to the circus monkey that whips the others into rocking horse and somersaults.

"She is domineering," Vivi says of Jolie. "She orders the other dogs around—if a dog wants to go out, she won't let him. If a dog wants to get in, she growls. She never bites but she scares them. All the dogs respect her. I think she is insecure—she knows she is not the most beautiful, the most loved in life. She fusses in order to be noticed. She acts out the important role she'd like to have."

Passing through the hallway while Vivi takes me to the bedroom, I hear the dogs—in the living room, the kitchen, the terrace—whine, bark, compete, scratch at the door. I see them jump up and down at some window, the taller over the shorter, to catch a glimpse of us, attract Vivi's attention, perchance her pity, and oh! the joyful yelps to be let out. The tallest, Darling, usually wins at the window. It is her black nose and the tips of her black ears that I get to see from out on the terrace where laundry dries under the hot Haiti sun.

"Darling is cumbersome," Vivi says. "She is noisy. She attacks.

I don't like her temperament. But she is very affectionate with me and needs love too. She used to sleep in the bedroom but since Katia has been here she stays in the hallway at night—she hates Katia's children. She does not attack but she snarls and leaps back in horror at the mere sight of them. Darling is also very helpful at night during the rat hunt."

At midnight, Vivi turns all lights out and goes around blindly hitting walls with a stick.

The dogs wait silently with open jaws, hanging tongues, and wagging tails. Once a rat comes out, the dogs screech, scream, howl, bite, and dash with competitive thrill. When a dog catches the rat, it groans with gleeful greed, agitates the raucous rodent in its clenched jaws, and then parades it high like it were a bleeding ball at the tip of a SeaWorld otter's nose.

Clown-faced Katia waits out in the bathroom with her sons, Titus and Brutus, who were born there. She won't let them play.

"When I was a child, you used to rescue rats," I say, "no matter how angry that made Father. He'd set the traps and you'd go behind him to take the cheese bit away. If a rat got into his chamber pot full of piss under the bed and could not get back out, come morning, you would pour them all out at the back of the house—live rat and piss. Now you set the dogs after the rats. How come?"

"We change. I don't like rats any more. I am afraid of them."

In the end, I never know how many dogs Vivi has. The thing is, she keeps dogs in two other places as well.

One place is at Hector's, a tall, soft hunk of a friend who worked as a masseur. Hector has become hunger-skinny. It's over the massages that Vivi and Hector became friends. He likes dogs and does not mind keeping Vivi's overflow in the back of the tiny corner store he now owns.

If a dog at Hector's is good at making Vivi feel that life is unbearable without her, she'll take it back.

That's what Katia did.

"Every time I'd leave," Vivi says, "Katia would sit on her bottom, open wide her eyes like windows and tell me, 'Adopt me

Mommy; I am not happy here; I want to go with you.' How can I resist that white-whiskered face of hers? She is both a seal and a squirrel."

As soon as Katia hears her name she is right there in front of us, floored rear end, flap-flapping tail, window eyes.

"Look," Vivi says, "how she closes her eyes when she gets a kiss—she tastes it just like she does her pussy when she cleans it. That, she treats like a precious jewel. And she should—their sex is very pretty, a little flower, a true button. It's prettier than women's. Noisette is like that too. You couldn't touch her pussy until she was nine years old and fell in love with Kali. He is dead now."

Noisette, a yellow dog who only loves Vivi, hides underneath a chair every time I am at the house. She stares at Vivi the whole time until I leave. The way Vivi stares at *me* today, I see that she too wants me to leave.

"Vivi? I must tell you . . ."

"No! I won't hear about it. If you have time to waste today, what you should do instead is to read what Voltaire wrote on dogs' loyalty. You'll learn about dogs of one person only. They lie on your grave and wait for death rather than accept another master. They know how to suffer. Noisette here, I picked up on Rue Clerveau when I lived in Pétion-Ville. It was midnight. I heard her cry and bark—a big dog was trying to rape her. She must have been five months old. I ran down the street in my bathrobe. She let me pick her up without making a fuss. The security guard next door refused to help me. In this country, people believe that, at night, dogs are *bakas* or some other manifestation of witchcraft. Noisette is a mistrustful loner. Rightfully so. Her whole life is to be near me. You see, happiness for a dog is to be with her master. Even without a roof. But there is master and *master*, mind you! You have to caress them, talk to them. A dog must feel loved. I must admit that mine are not dogs anymore. They are spoiled rotten, ill-mannered kids—Noisette refuses to eat if there is no meat. She can spend three weeks sulking and I have to force her spoonful by spoonful. Do you understand what I am trying to tell you?"

"Yes."

"See here? You can tell a dog's health by the color inside its ears. My dogs are healthy. When they are not, I won't sleep until they are cured. There was this yellow dog—Salamander, I called him—who got sick and needed five suppositories a day: one before breakfast, one during breakfast, one after breakfast, one before lunch and one after dinner. I was turned into a vigilant suppository nursemaid. He lived to be eighteen."

"Did you use rubber gloves to insert them?"

"What for?"

The other place where Vivi keeps dogs is at Wilson's. "Wilson, he's got muscle!" she says with admiration. She may have a tender heart for runts, cripples, and wounded dogs, but when it comes to men they've got to be big, strong, and with all their fingers. "And after fifteen years, Wilson is family. Ten children, he has. I have known all of them since they were babies. Besides, I don't want any female working for me. You know I don't like women."

"How about your female dogs?"

"It's different—they are dogs. Coming back to Wilson, he is my assistant; I taught him. He can dress wounds, repair broken legs, give shots, even to me. I lift my skirt and I tell him 'Go ahead.' Mercy shots too. We use my own recipe. He is invaluable. Haitians don't usually like animals. But him, you have to see how he scouts the hills looking for dogs, goats, pigs, even roosters, anything that hurts."

"No cats?"

"Cats don't get time to roam—they get eaten. You know that."

"How can you be sure Wilson really scouts the hills?"

"What are you insinuating? You think he lies to me? You should hear how animals scream in the slums across the river. People vent their frustrations and throw rocks at anything that walks on four. Human beings? They're shit. Animals only attack if you hurt them. People do harm as a sport."

Vivi is loyal to Wilson and, vexed, pouts a bit. It doesn't last—she doesn't hold grudges and loves to chat.

"But listen, I haven't told you the best one yet: The other day, Wilson tells me there is a nursing mother dog with a deep, infected wound on her foot. The poor beast is tied to a stick by the river, with worms eating and going up her leg. She is as good as dead. Wilson and I went with my whole pharmacy to treat the dog right there by the water. Women and children dropped their laundry to come watch and they laughed at us. They think I belong in a madhouse—sending Wilson around to police them as soon as I hear a dog holler. I am right on the other side of the river—I hear everything. You wouldn't believe the scandals going on. I just turn the TV up to drown the noise—they can kill each other off if they want, but not dogs. Anyway, Wilson made room in his house for the mama-dog that gets along fine with his other dogs: wife, children, dogs, and Mama Dog, all of them in but three rooms in the slums. When the dog gets well, the owner suddenly shows up to claim her. In the meantime, I had paid for Mama Dog's food, medicine, bandages and all. Wilson tells the owner he has to contribute. He says, 'OK, but I'll reimburse you after I come back from the provinces. I must be off to take care of some business and, by the way, would you keep these two puppies in the meantime?' So now, there are three more at Wilson's. Such a good heart this Wilson. No two like him."

Three times a week, Vivi goes on routes to visit the dogs for which she has found homes. She brings them treats and, in the homes where people are poor, she brings them food. If a dog is mistreated, she takes it back. When a dog dies, she grieves like a child.

Recent dogs that have died at home were Alexandre, Tcha-Tcha, Pataud, Moustique, and even a Vivi. Their graves are in the garden, surrounding my father's.

Dogs' graves are circular mounds of earth marked by crosses fashioned with two sticks held together with cut-up bits of Vivi's old scarves. Father hated dogs in all manner of shapes, colors and sizes. He hated them for the dog shit he stepped on in his garden. Hated them for being unsightly strays that licked his wife's hands that fed them *his* food. But he did buy Darling, a Doberman, in Miami, for a lot of money. He went on and on about how she was a pedigreed dog, the real thing; how Doberman females are fierce, obedient, and they, at least, are loyal to the death.

Father and Mother had that in common—they were disloyal to each other but loved the loyalty they believed to be found in dogs.

But a month was not over before Darling, still a puppy, started with diarrhea that stained Father's mosaic floors. He brought her to Vivi who, since their divorce, lived penniless in Pétion-Ville. Vivi took Darling back to him after the diarrhea was gone. Until the next diarrhea, and the next, and my father could not stand "that she-dog" any more and Darling too shifted loyalty. Vivi no longer lives in Pétion-Ville. The place she now inhabits is actually the finished top third floor of my father's unfinished house, which she calls the "castle" and whose completion his accidental death put to an abrupt end.

The "castle" is built right by the river that runs at the foot of the hill on top of which our original family home stood. Vivi was grateful that I asked her to come back to the land where she had lived so many years of her life during her marriage and where, in a sense, she had grown up alongside her daughter.

"I am convinced that he realizes now the loving companionship dogs provide and enjoys having them around in the other world," Vivi says to me.

"You forget this is the man you were terrified would sneak around your Pétion-Ville house at night to poison your dogs? And there were only four or five at the time!"

When Vivi was still in Pétion-Ville, the purple bandages around her fingers were not covering dog bites but stress-related eczema.

And now, shit in the garden is an ongoing issue. "Shit is organic and flies have to live too," she says to me when I complain about it. This is not to say that Vivi is careless about cleanliness, but she concentrates on the house. In fact, most days, the mosaic floor looks like it is just recovering from a detergent flood. In the hallways, the dogs are careful not to slip and hesitate to speed.

Avocado and mango trees around Vivi's place reach up to the third floor. Early morning, she sits naked under the top branches of those hanging over her balcony, lost in bird songs and blue sky. When she gets up from her reverie, she hoses the dogs and herself down. The dogs jump up and down to catch the water jet in their jaws. The joy she feels by playing with them reminds her of being a child.

"I was a bagful of tricks," Vivi says of her French childhood vacations at the manor house in Puyraveaux, an area of Vendée.

"Having to sleep in the basement with the rats was punishment for playing ghost and scaring an old lady who was visiting."

She laughs and her eyes dance.

"Before the war, in my grandmother's attic in Vésinet, there were wonderful trunks full of old frills and costumes. I got myself all dressed up and dreamt of all sorts of wonderful lives I'd have. In Puyraveaux, there were only white sheets for dress-up. I had a friend, Roger, son of the florist in Sartrouville, my hometown. He came to Puyraveaux too. We climbed on trees—to the top! Trees are my passion, more so than flowers. Flowers are beautiful but I don't like to see them cut. Trees have their heads in the sky."

"What happened to Roger?"

"He got married, became a naturalist and stuffed birds. Man kills everything—birds, flowers, name it—and afterwards they either stuff it or make plastic reproductions. I guess it's still a kind of afterlife? Roger had given me one of these birds. But in Haiti insects ate it up, like they will everything else."

The wonderful afterlife dog companionship she talks about in relation to my dead father is actually what she hopes for herself, after her funeral whose elaborate ritual is very well described in any of her wills, all of them handwritten at night during insomnia on pages torn from schoolchildren's copy books. She mails the will to me or lets me know where she hides it. There is never a lawyer involved.

"Lawyers! The hell with lawyers! Yesterday, today, or tomorrow!" she laughs at me.

Vivi's layout for burial is modeled exactly after her bedtime ritual with the dogs.

"I want you to kill all my dogs and bury them with me," she writes, "because they could not be happy anywhere else."

When Vivi gets ready to sleep, she lies down with dogs tucked all around her body. Each dog knows its exact allotted space and which of Vivi's limbs is its territory: Harmonie lies behind Vivi's head, resting her chin on Vivi's forehead, her healthy dog's cold nose seen right above Vivi's; Nino lies under Vivi's right arm; Venus comes right after Nino, at Vivi's waist; Puce is at her thigh;

then comes Jolie at her calf while Somalie and Noisette each curl around one foot; Katia and her three children, Melodie, Titus, and Brutus, take up the other side of Vivi's body. The bedroom being an extension of Vivi's body as well, the rest of the dogs who are not honored enough to receive a place on the bed go off and select either open floor space or the canopy of chairs and table. Sophie and Papito are downstairs on the first floor. They serve as gate-keepers because they don't get along with anyone but each other.

"What do you do if you need to get up in the night?" I ask.

"I don't."

"Even if it hurts?"

"I make sacrifices for my dogs. I want them to be happy and safe. I want to make up for what Life did to them. Nino was a starved, white pup I untied from a lamppost and Jolie was picked up out of a pothole. Venus was saved from a beggar who kept her in a pillowcase. Somalie and Puce were half-drowned fleabags lifted off the riverbank mucus after a big rain. Even Harmonie was a street reject! My languorous Harmonie! My harem girl. My friend Nancy had put her out in the street. Six months old. Bad karma for Nancy—she is dead. Her husband hurried up and married some woman with whom he already had a little girl. It suited everyone that Nancy died. She used to put a pillow in bed between her husband and her. That was the signal that he wasn't supposed to cross over. At first she put it once in a while, and then a little more often. In the end it was every night and in the morning the bed was made up with the pillow rooted in the middle."

Remembering her friend whose death no one mourned, Vivi stays quiet for a while. But she soon speaks again.

"There were no dogs in my childhood," she says, "except for one, Barry, my father's German shepherd. Barry got lost in the crowd when we were fleeing the Germans on our way to Puyraveaux in Vendée. Our car was packed tight so Barry was coming with Madame Olcèse, the housekeeper, on foot. Poor Barry. He must have starved to death. Every dog of my life connects me to my first dog and is an extension of him."

"I understand."

"No, you don't."

"Alright . . ."

"I remember it all like it was yesterday. The past is a hungry animal I feed with memories . . . It helps and it hurts too. The past is good and gone. But without my memory, I don't exist."

"Memory of dogs?"

Vivi gives me a disdainful side glance.

"You should not have come," she says.

"I had to, considering what happened . . . By the way, isn't your birthday coming soon?"

"What? Ah yes . . ." Vivi looks startled. She turns her face away as her eyes drift in the distance. "Never mind what happened . . ." she says again. "These neighbors are like rats busying their little rodents' minds. My dogs are not doing the barking at night—they sleep with me. It's the slum dogs who bark because they are tied without food or water."

"I am just glad you don't go and add those to your collection when you should be thinking about cutting down instead."

Vivi turns a frowning face back toward me. "I decide what's good for me," she says.

"The result is now a big mess."

"No one is asking you."

"Yes, *they* are . . ."

"My dogs, at least, are not waiting to see me dead like *they* are."

"Can Wilson help you with your bandages?"

"I don't need help. I can take care of myself. I am not yet dead."

Vivi sits down. I walk to her and sit on the bed next to her. I place my hand on hers. "What was it?" I ask softly. "How did it happen? Did you forget the oven was on? Shouldn't we go to a dermatologist?"

"My father was a doctor. I know how to treat burns. Let me be."

"You speak to me as if I were your enemy. You refuse to see . . ."

"See what?" she says and gets up with agitation. She makes a sweeping gesture with open arms that seem to encompass all that is vast and invisible. "This world is a zoo!"

"This *house* is a zoo."

"That's it then—you want to put me in a cage too? You want my death!"

"*Your* death? It's always all about you! Have you thought of the sort of death you are putting on *me*? You want me to get rid of your dogs after you die? Kill them for you? And who will protect *my* memory of this pharaoh's funeral of yours you are planning for me to give you? Who will help *my* memory carry the load of that massacre? You say I hate dogs. I don't. I love dogs. But I am afraid of *your* dogs—each new dog represents the weight of one more murder for me. It should be burden enough to lose one's mother!"

Vivi looks at me with silent eyes, then comes back to sit next to me. "I just have a few years left to live and I should feel guilty about you *having* to bury me?" she says.

"I need to keep remembering that *you* are the mad playwright here or else I will go mad, right here, right now—you wrote this farce, you created all the characters, the dogs, your memory, your fears, the trees, the rats, me even, you created me, your daughter, the unwilling accomplice, miserable witness of this day."

"You hate me because I don't live the way that would be comfortable for you. You want me to bake apple pies, wear frilly aprons and high-collared dresses. You want me to resemble you—neat, tucked, and quiet—and live like you do. But you won't win. This, here, is not my daughter."

"Some days, I wish I were not. But, there's still the matter of your neighbors. It's not just the dog-barking, it's also the dog-biting now. That is why the process server gave me the paper to hand it to you. He couldn't get to your door. Barry ran after him, possessed most likely by the spirit of your childhood dog."

"Excellent!" Vivi chuckles.

She takes a couple of big cushions from behind her back and puts them behind mine. She tries to make me lean back and insists that I would be more comfortable.

"I hope he bit his ass to bits," she says.

"Did not."

"Too bad."

"Not so. If Barry had bitten him, the neighbors would have had a stronger case."

"They're already *strong*."

"No. You can fight back if you make some changes. Why don't you ever open your own mail?"

"Stop the questioning and stop plotting against my dogs!" she says, getting back up again. She walks to the commode and, coming back, readjusts the position of a dog figurine. She places it closer to center. She then goes to the chair nearby and changes its direction as well, pulling it back more, further from me.

"I am only trying to tell you that in this mad world you complain about, there are still efforts at sanity that can be made. Even by using the law. Even in Haiti."

Vivi sits down on the chair. While she must be readying her mind for a fight, she displays a defeated, helpless look instead. Her back rounds itself and her shoulders droop as if she were trying to fit herself into an invisible cocoon.

"Forgive me," she cries. "It's not my fault. I have been hounded since I was a child: I have to dress like everybody and wear navy blue, grays, and browns. No red, no apple green, no color that plays or sings. They want to put a lid on me. I must be a mouse. I want to dance and they want me to sit with my legs tight shut. The world suffocates me. My mother and my husband more than anyone. You understand? All I have now are my dogs. That is all I have. I choose dogs over people. Don't you know?"

"I know."

"I read about the Jim Crow era in America when they decided that black people were three-fifths human. What do you think of it? Not so bad? Three-fifths is more than just halfway there? Jesus . . . Can you imagine grown people seriously trying to *analyze* what percentage of human attributes other human beings have? And it's *me* they call crazy. Now, what percentage human do you think dogs are? One-fifth? Two-fifths? As far as I am concerned, my dogs are six-fifths human! Look into their eyes— more human than humans! If I had the choice I'd rather be my dog than myself."

"And me?"

"You have your life. I would die if anything happened to you. But, for the dogs, I *am* everything."

"You are everything for me too. I am like one of your dogs. When you suffer, I suffer. I envy your dogs that they may die rather than have to live without you."

"Oh la la la la, what melodrama!"

"I envy your dogs that they are everything for you. Even the ones in memory."

"Where is your good sense!"

"I envy those dogs that they have my mother."

"We need some air!" she says, getting up. "Open the windows! Kick out those thoughts right now."

"Yes . . ."

"And don't meddle in my memories," she says as she turns toward me from the window where she is now standing. She points a finger at me. "Besides, it is not just the mind that remembers, you know. Our body is also full of memories. Every cell of ours is a coffer of a kind." She now points the finger to the sky and shakes it a bit as if she were taking God Himself as a witness and making sure she gets His attention. "My body remembers every limb of the dog Barry that waited for my parents to go to sleep before he would crawl up my bed to lie on top of me. He guarded me. He loved me. He was my friend. And his life was treated with less value than clothes or cooking pots were, because there was no room saved for him in our car when we left. My dogs are my memory. If you kill them, you kill me."

"Mother . . ."

"Call me Vivi! You sound like I should sound and yet I don't. I am the old lady here, not you. I was once beautiful and men courted me like crazy. Not a single lover is left now. My legs hurt. My whole body hurts. But I wake in the morning and swell up my lungs. I want to live!" she says in a cry and swirls with open arms, her face lifted to heaven. Then she stops short and looks at me. "My father taught me about that. He was all heart my Papa, and a great doctor. He fought in the French underground and was decorated after the war. We saved lots of American pilots and hid them in the attic. One of them gave me my first cigarette. They called my mother 'la belle blonde.' I taught them that, for a joke, and they taught me how to smoke. Yes . . . Those were the days, even if it was the war . . . But . . . Who is barking like that? And, where are the dogs?! There is just Noisette that's here under the chair . . . even Harmonie is not on the bed! *Mon Dieu!*"

Vivi rushes out of the bedroom forgetting that her legs don't obey such fast commands any longer. She almost slips on a fresh pee puddle but I am right behind to catch her by the waist in time.

"*Mon Dieu!* The dogs are all gone! Wilson must have come

over and heard us talk—he decided he'd come back later and just hooked the padlock over the bars instead of locking it well. But no—the dogs couldn't have lifted up the padlock, even if it's loose, or, at least, we would have heard them rattling it . . . And who opened the door to the terrace? And the kitchen door? *Mon Dieu!* I have to catch them. Oh la la . . . Come with me. Hurry!"

"I am right here."

Vivi grabs the rat stick from a side table and hurries down the stairs while admonishing her knees that they "had better hold and this is not the time to give out."

Sophie and Papito live in an enclosed area accessed through a small gate at the bottom of the stairs next to the garage. It is a good alert station against anything or anyone that may want to go up the stairs. Wilson is the only one, besides Vivi, who they will not bark at, bite, or even eat alive if given half a chance. Right now they are so heated up and dizzy from barking away, part giving alert and part jealousy at all the dogs they watched earlier slip down the stairs and out past them, that they even bark at Vivi and bare their teeth at her.

Sophie, a smooth, all-white female whose immaculate looks, Vivi says, would make you give her "communion without confess," is actually the meanest of dogs and sets the tone for Papito, who emulates all she does. She snarls and drools and barks all at the same time, the fur along her spine standing up straight, hard, bone-like and almost red it so reflects and moves from her fury.

"Enough!" Vivi barks back at Sophie, hitting the flat of her head with the stick, and then she speeds along to chase after her bastard horde of happy, furry escapees.

She is wearing her emerald-green satin robe that reaches down to her ankles.

It is early evening now and the moon is already well drawn into the sky's darkening page. It allows the satin of the robe to glow with a grayish luster that makes her wide, ruffle-edged collar seem like it's her halo that has lain down on her shoulders. Her slippers, a gift from me, decorated with silver moon-sliver smiles and golden sun-discs, are not meant for a race in the night, and they flap uneasily and noisily under her heels; not thick enough for the ground's occasional gravel or pebble, they also cause Vivi to trip and blurt an "ouch" here and there.

But passion does not stop: going through the circular garden where my father's grave stands, I watch her as she brandishes her stick and calls out each dog by its name while the evening sea breeze swells up her robe as if it wants to transport her.

I feel like the Sancho Panza of a demented Merlin caught in an enchanted ring where mad lions, Sophie and Papito, bark ceaselessly, joined by a mad gargoyle, Katia, who turns out to be on the lookout above on the upstairs terrace.

Like Noisette does, Katia remembers fearfully the world out there and is using up all her voice both to support my mother and to order Titus and Brutus back home.

"What are *you* doing here?" Vivi asks.

I turn to see who she is addressing. It is Wilson's son, also called Wilson.

He must be six years old and his mother is already dead. He adores Vivi. Deprived of attention and of toys, he likes to follow his father, unnoticed, going from bush to bush. Being so small and black-skinned, it is easy for him to hide in this moonlit night.

But his eyes themselves are like two moons as he stares at Vivi from behind a tree trunk where he stands.

"So you're the one who let the dogs out!?"

Moon-silence.

"Where is your father?"

Moon-silence.

"Wilson!" She orders Wilson, "Go get Wilson!"

Wilson does not move. The moons blink, that's all. The boy looks terrified at what he has unleashed.

"He is just a child," I tell her.

"Just a child, just a child, nevertheless he's put me in deep shit. It's the neighbors that are going to be grunting with glee now."

With that, she turns away to continue calling the dogs, and suddenly notices: "Damn! And the gate is open too! They've really made an escape. There is nothing like stolen fun. It's going to be some sport to get them back in."

The first to come and look is Darling, wearing a grin. She is wagging her tail at the stick, thinking this is an outdoor rat hunt. As soon as she realizes that Vivi is trying to get ahold of her, she makes a turn about-face and bolts faster than if she were on wheels, long pink tongue flapping out on the side of a persistent grin all fresh in the breeze. Then we notice Barry behind a tree, scratching the ground with his hind legs like he is distractedly throwing dirt on something.

"Barry! Come here!"

He comes, reluctantly, but also wearing the Darling grin. He's got a light step like he has accomplished something meaningful and is proud of himself. Barry does not mind being grabbed at—he is not wearing a collar and it is no sweat for him to just pull away and destabilize Vivi, who again almost falls before I grab her.

"Thank you!" she says, laughing. "The *dog*! He tricked me. He is clever. But, first things first, we have to close the gate . . ."

"I'll do it."

"You go ahead. I am right behind you. My legs slow me down. Leave a crack open so I can call them from there. You hide to the side. If that Wilson's Wilson weren't so moonstruck he might be able to help us. Just the two of us is not enough."

"Better me than no one."

"Well, yes. OK. Once we trap them back in the yard, it will be easier to get them in the house. At any rate, they'll eventually get tired and want to sleep. Right now, the moonlight's on; the fun has just begun."

In fact, as Vivi's and my own eyes get accustomed to the dim light, we see that the dogs are all in view and all wearing the Darling grin.

"Max! Somalie!"

Each time Vivi calls a name, she is answered by the anxious Mother Gargoyle and by the two lions.

"Jolie!"

Bark! Bark-bark!

"Nino!"

Bark! Bark-bark!

But the one being called responds not by barking and then obeying the call, as hoped for, but by a sudden jerking motion, or some whip-a-doo dance with frivolous flap of plumed tail, or by a merry-go-round chase of one after the other, specially Titus and Brutus, or again by a forward taunting trot immediately followed by a cavorting retreat with a look back to see the effect of the performance.

At some point, Vivi sends me to attempt to get past them so I can try to shoo them back in from the rear. But, feathered and free as they seem, like prancing horses in a circus parade of glistening mane under the moon's spotlight, they are not chicken and shooing does not work.

So Vivi tells me to hide and station myself back at the side of the gate. She tries to hide herself next to me and stay silent to see if the dogs will worry or be curious enough to come and look for her.

The dogs respond to Vivi's maneuver like she is in the game with them as in the midnight rat hunt. Indeed, Harmonie and Melodie and Puce eventually do suddenly whiz past us through the gate, one behind the other, panting, but as soon as they notice us standing there hidden and the gate being quickly shut, they just about make a gymnast's backward flip and somehow, while Vivi and I try to grab onto one, the other two flatten themselves enough to slip back out in the narrow space under the gate and then bark, the other dogs outside the gate joining in the barking, creating enough disturbance that, in the commotion, the third dog rips herself from our hands, makes a run for it, slips under and gets away the same flat way.

"Well! What an act!" I say. "Maybe we could train the animals to jump *over* the gate now."

Vivi does not answer—perhaps it's the sudden cool breeze that lifts and causes her to fold her skinny arms, as if she is closing in, and open over her shivering breast her long, arthritic fingers that look like gnarled ginger roots.

The breeze then seems to swirl upward along tree trunks and the agitation in their dense foliage makes the soft sound of brooms sweeping, while the palm tree leaves, high above us, sway like the heart would if it could wave to the stars.

Her dogs are silent.

"They are waiting for me," Vivi says. "I'll go. You stay here."

Suddenly I become aware of the sounds in this night that paradoxically give the silence its density.

There are the unsteady, limping steps that my mother takes over the uneven ground past the gate, her hands now preceding her, touching the darkness as if they could better discern the landscape ahead than her eyes can, and as if, in this unaccustomed night, the rules and conditions for her senses were new. The moon draws flowing, luminous eyes on her old satin robe like it does on coursing water and makes it look wet as it clings to the flimsiness of the body beneath it, the body that moves in it, hardly a body at all, so frail, I notice, too brittle to be thought evanescent while it eludes definition, beyond all caresses.

I hear the little river running nearby. It is too late an hour to speak of chatter in the water; yet it is convincingly the sound of language, but the kind that increases aloneness rather than addresses your being.

I feel rather than see the spark of distant fires and hear the barking of dogs far in the hills like echoes of the past lives that Vivi narrates. I lift my face to the night air and try to find my mother's scent in it. I think I recognize her perfume, but is it already, I wonder, only my memory of it?

Meat

With three bullets stuck in his chest and still in his chair, the dead watchman at the downtown Port-au-Prince Bridgestone store got his shoes stolen from his feet less than three minutes after the *zenglendo* thieves killed him so they could rob the place for whatever small amount of cash was in the register. In Haiti now, there isn't much time for sentiment. It didn't take long for someone walking by the storefront to take one look at that still-warm dead watchman to figure out he wouldn't need his shoes any longer. Better take them now than leave them for some of the corpse's relatives to have. Besides, the watchman may not have any relative those shoes would fit. We've got to be sensible. I come from a country of coconuts. Fate is like a coconut—you never know when it's gonna fall. Can be good, can be bad. If it falls on your head, tough luck. If it falls at your feet, you've got something sweet to eat, something sweet to drink. That's what happened with the shoe story—the watchman got it on the head, the man passing by got it at his feet. You see, this coconut business has made us a fatalistic people. We take what comes and we make sensible choices.

Talking about sensible choices: you see me sitting here with you—a nice young woman—in this Miami airport? I'm waiting for the next plane home because I just missed mine. Why did I miss my plane? Because of some excess baggage I was trying to put in someone else's who offered I do that because he had very little baggage of his own and I had way too much. Was going to cost me a fortune. After I put some of mine in his, I started redoing my packing so I could spread the weight differently. I didn't realize it took so long, and by the time I got to the boarding gate, they'd just closed it and given my seat to someone on standby. Anyway, I was talking about sensible choices, right? Well, what do you think all that weight is about anyway? Gifts you say? You are right! But what kind of gifts d'you think? Don't even bother to answer. I'll tell you right now: it's not scarves, doilies, or smart books. It's meat. I bring meat.

And meat weighs. Specially the frozen ones. The cooked ones not as much obviously. And meat is what we need. Meat to eat so we can put some meat on our bones. If you looked at our people and didn't know better, you'd think it's the sun that melts away the meat from the bones. Some people are nasty enough to say that we dance and fornicate so much that the meat never has a chance to stick. I tell you though, I'm not the only one that lugs meat every time I get a chance to go home.

Meat is crisscrossing America all over and every day in Haitians' baggage. Oversized, overstuffed, overused baggage that tears, bursts, explodes all over the runways, or sometimes stands there; and I say stand, not sit, because it's not the kind that sits—it has bulk, it has presence, it has legs it stands on and challenges you to move it if you dare. It's like a donkey that won't go forward no matter what and everybody behind you in the line helps pushing at it just so they get their turn and don't miss the plane.

I tell you, they hate us at the airports. They hire special people for us—to keep Haitians in a single line, quietly one behind the other. Maybe it's thinking about us that someone thought of that cellophane-luggage-wrap machine. Maybe they'd love to wrap us just like that—neatly and tightly. Everything has to be so neat and controlled all the time. And straight! And you know there ain't nothing straight enough about us. We are here on this earth to illustrate the meaning of curve—look! My nose, my hair, my ass. Our emotions also have too much curve! They swell and wave, they bulge in our chest, burst from all our movements. We're overwhelming and overwhelmed, we're dislocated and desperate, disorderly and often illiterate, but! MEAT, we know how to pack.

You can freeze it like a rock and it will take the whole day you're traveling to defrost, and your relatives will cook it that same night if they don't have a fridge—that's one. Two is the way you prepare the meat so it can last several days without spoiling—sometimes Port-au-Prince isn't your last stop even though half the family has been there waiting for you all day on those airport benches because waiting for someone they love is fun and because they came far from the provinces anyway, traveling by bus day and night, and they have no place else to wait. And that place far in the provinces is where that cooked meat is gonna have to go before any relative gets to chew any piece of it. Me, I'm going to Chantal. That's where my mother is and that's where I grew up. So, from Port-au-Prince I have to take the bus to Les Cayes, and from there, find some kind of a ride to Chantal. All the meat I've got now stored in the plane's belly is gonna go to my mother's belly.

I've got goat, beef, lamb, and chicken. It's all cooked—I won't get to Chantal before tomorrow night. The meat is all prepared. I'll tell you how I do it. Everybody does it this way. Ask any Haitian woman that travels with meat, and she'll tell it to you the same. So, first the meat needs to soak in salt and vinegar. Beforehand, I poke and slice it to let the salt and vinegar get in real good. Then, I prepare spices to marinate the meat—leek, parsley, salt, Maggi cubes, garlic, onion, hot pepper. Afterwards, I take the meat, wash it with sour oranges, rub all the spices on it. At this point, the meat is ready to be cooked, under low heat, covered, so it loses most of its juices, but not all. Don't add any oil, or any liquid of any kind—heat and spices will make the meat sweat. After that treatment, nothing can happen to it: nothing can hurt it, nothing can spoil it. Your meat's safe.

The way I have it figured out, my mother and my relatives will enjoy meat for at least a week. I know they haven't had any since the last time I visited. You hear about this food chain story? Well, Haitians aren't at the top of it like the rest of the beautiful people in this world. We go up and down. Sometimes we're up on it like when I go home with the meat. Other times it's the other animals that make it to the top feeding on us. These days, sharks eat us. When we're shot to death and left on the ground to rot, it's ants and worms that eat us. When we get dumped in the sewage, it's rats that get fat on us. Their beady eyes get all shiny on that human vitamin. If we happen to make it to some proper burial, the cockroaches are on standby. I know you don't agree with this kind of reasoning, but me, that's the way I see it and that's that. Mind you, I've got my reasons—my youngest brother, it's the rats that were enjoying his sweet seventeen-year-old meat. We were looking everywhere for him—the hospital, the police, the morgue. Some woman watching her steps at night for uncovered sewage holes saw something big that was floating. She called the police. My little brother was so swollen they could not lift him outta there. Picks and shovels got him out of that black piss and pulp of God-knows-what. The rats were sorry.

And he hadn't done a thing. He wasn't in any kind of politics. Not that there isn't anything to complain about and be in politics for, mind you.

He was walking downtown and some guys picked him up. Don't know who, don't know why. They beat him to death, dumped him. My mother fainted at the morgue. First drawer they pull open, it's him—her baby. Still now, it's been fifteen years, if she hears his name mentioned, she can't eat for days. She had thirteen children; only four of us are left. Two of us here. I'm in Boston. My sister's in New Hampshire. She should be here with me today.

I'm going to my father's funeral. That's why I'm wearing all black. It's not for fun I'm going to Haiti this time. He died Thursday. I'm ashamed my sister isn't here with me. She's never been back since she left. She's afraid. Today is Saturday. She says she'll come Monday. She won't. I told her to give me the money of the trip, that way I can distribute it to relatives. She says she'll send it if she can't come. Lies. They are sick of seeing me down there. Every year I go. Even my mother says what's wrong with me, I keep coming back. They've waited at the airport all morning and they're going to be sorry it's me not her. Me, with these seven identical black hats piled up on my head for all of us women of the family to wear at the funeral. My father will be proud. Death reunites us. But really, we shouldn't wait for death to do that.

He was sick and we knew he wouldn't last long. Cancer. Cancer killed him. Cancer all over. Can you picture this: my father's body eating itself up? What a mess when the doctor opened him up! All his insides turned into ground meat. The doctor closed him without touching a thing. Too late. I told you he died Thursday? Right. Well, ever since Monday I have felt as if my bones were broken. My relatives may be sick of seeing me but I know my father wants to see me. How do I know that? It's clear—because when they called me to tell me he was dead, I couldn't move. I was dead. Neighbors gave me bitter coffee—didn't work. It's only after I talked with him I was able to move. No, I didn't light a candle. What? No, I didn't make any promises. I just talked to him, I told him: Help me, give me strength, because if you don't I won't be able to go to your funeral, and I want to go; help me. It worked right away! If it weren't for that I wouldn't be sitting in Miami airport talking to you to pass the time. Do I feel sorrow? No. I don't feel these things any more. I used to. Had bad thoughts too. Once, I stood in front of a train track. I wanted to let my body drop on the tracks. Neighbors told me to pray—ask God to remove these thoughts from my head. So now, that's what I do. If you die, I just don't think of you anymore. My father's dead. After the funeral, I won't think of him anymore.

Besides, I have enough stuff that fills up my head. I have three children, two of them twins. Luck? Yes, I hear twins bring luck. Mine don't. Maybe it works if you have two boys or two girls. I have one of each. And they fight. And neighbors fight. Even Spirits fight! In the neighborhood where I live, things have gotten so bad no one trusts anyone anymore. It could get just like it is in Haiti now, where neighbors throw stones at each other, and if it's not hungry people piled on top of each other in one room under a tin roof like in a steam bath, it's the dogs getting at each other when they can't find a goat to gang up on.

You think I'm making this up? Let me tell you. You know how in Haiti people like to have dogs to watch the house but they don't like to feed them? What d'you say? Yes, that's true—they can't feed them. Anyway, just the other day in Chantal, some dogs killed and ate a man's goat. The man was so frustrated—his only goat! All day long he went after all the dogs in the neighborhood, guilty or not guilty, and hacked them to death with his machete. Some weren't quite sliced enough and died only after they had lost all their blood. D'you know how many dogs died in Haiti that day? A mess I tell you. And we don't eat dogs. An angry waste— that's what it was if you ask me.

And you think that's the only sickness going around now? It isn't. I have a brother . . . What? What brother? Never mind what brother. I tell you, this one or that one, they're all my brothers. All Haitians are my brothers. What's more—everybody in the world's my brother. My mother, your mother, her mother, it's all the same belly! And that's what can drive you crazy—what's happening to you or him over there, it's happening to me. Like those quilts in Maine they call crazy quilts—made up of all kinds of fabrics, all sizes, all colors, stitched together—you know, and if one place gets torn or damaged, any other piece of fabric can replace it, because all the flowers, same blanket? Well, all the red blood going around—same thing, same blanket. See what I mean? Anyway, I was telling you about my brother and his sickness. He is getting old, my brother, and it's around the mouth it's showing. His lips used to be full and soft; now they're getting small and cracked. His father didn't love him, and his mother, well, she had others to take care of. It's like he is drying up where he couldn't suck or scream. And now all he wants is little girls. He is horny for little girls. Ten years old and his eyes get funny when he looks at them. He thinks they're looking at him too. Fifty-five years old he is! He tells me a five-year-old once grabbed his balls knowing full well what she was doing. He says I don't know what's going on in the world any more and if my twelve-year-old says she is still a virgin it's either a lie or I don't give her enough rope, and whatever she don't do for fun, she'll do for money. So I tell him that a little girl is not a piece of meat, that the head needs time to catch up with the body, it's not because a fruit has color it's ripe to be eaten, and then I tell him about love, love that can save us all, that love's the Messiah, that my man's love is waiting for me at home like a Messiah, my Messiah, my man is, and I tell my brother, I tell him, and he looks at me like I am crazy.

Land

JUSTIN

The day I stood naked under the midday sun with two land crabs Djezèl put on top of my head, there were a good twenty snakes sunning themselves in the fig tree behind me. Villagers say these tree-loungers were real people Djezèl put spells on and turned into snakes. They claim he works for greedy clients who want to appropriate land illegally and pay him great sums to get the owners out of the way by any means he can. I don't believe that.

Even if he is a powerful Vodou priest who does magic "with both hands," good or evil magic, he would not destroy people.

Djezèl would not kill. Djezèl has a conscience. Besides, I know that fig tree is a shrine to Bossou and not some snake-zombies tree.

I did ask Djezèl, however, why he works two kinds of magic. He said, "It's God that created all and sees all. If something has happened, God somehow allowed it. Who am I to judge God's choices and decide what is good or bad? People come to me with their problems and I do what I can. The power I have, God allowed it."

I thought about what Djezèl said a lot until I stumbled on this proverb: "Bon Dye konn bay men li pa konn separe"— God gives all but He does not know how to split equally. I always gain peace from proverbs.

I guess we have to live and find our own justice. You can't wait for God to do everything. Besides, if I didn't trust Djezèl, I would not have asked him for an exorcism and put my whole life in his hands.

That is how I got to stand there naked, at noon sharp, with two red land crabs on my head.

Djezèl tied up their claws so they would not hurt me, but the crabs were restless and I could feel them trying to edge their carcasses out from the top of my head. These brainless creatures did not see that escape only meant a crashing six-foot fall onto the rocky earth where I stood.

I arrived early that morning in order to give Djezèl plenty of time to prepare everything. The crabs had to be ready to go at the strike of noon. By that time my stomach was growling, and the delicious, spicy smell from Djezèl's wife's *calalou gombo* left cooking on the open fire made my hunger more active. She had gotten everything set near the *mapou* tree.

Naturally prominent roots of the mapou make large enclaves above ground that look like canoes. Djezèl illuminates them on special nights. He makes small lamps out of sour oranges that are halved, emptied and left to dry under the sun. Then he fills them with lamp oil and sticks a cotton wick smack in the middle. He sets them on the ground inside the canoes.

You should see how they glow, like a family of small full moons! The moons shiver when there is a breeze.

While I stood there with the crabs on my head, Djezèl built a fire out of a tall pile of sticks that an *ounsi* had gathered from the eroded hills nearby. That ounsi is a pretty girl I have seen helping out during temple ceremonies many times.

Afterwards, he poured water on my head and whipped my whole body with fresh young branches taken from a *monben bata* tree. He kept praying continuously.

Then he suddenly grabbed one crab and threw it in the high flames. The live crab quickly grilled to a crisp. The ounsi picked up the remains of the crab and immediately ground it to a fine black powder. She then mixed it with other powders that Djezèl handed to her and that he had bought at a pharmacy in downtown Port-au-Prince.

Later on, he gave me that powder to use for healing the rash on my groin.

Speaking of the rash, Djezèl said it was caused by "bad air" I caught, some spell not meant for me, just by walking on land where I was not supposed to be. There must be some proverb that warns about being careful where one sets one's feet. So many proverbs in Haiti! There is always one for everything people do or should not do.

But I am not so sure the "bad air" was not meant for me, especially if I consider all my other problems besides the rash and the people harassing me at the time.

Besides, I walk all over the place and everybody knows that. Still, my mother declared the rash was from stress and looked like the eczema she has had on her fingers and toes all her life, on and off. An old doctor friend of hers whom she asked the favor of looking at my groin gave the rash a long medical name in Latin and handed me some ointment that cured nothing.

The second crab was picked up off of my head and released at the nearest crossroads.

It's amazing: in this country where there are too many people and you can never be alone—whenever you sit down along the road in the countryside for a few minutes, thinking you can be quietly by yourself, you soon realize there are many pairs of eyes watching you from the bushes before they come standing right in front of you with curiosity and ready questions—well, in that country, a crossroads always seems deserted, particularly if you need it for some ritual. People magically disappear from the crossroads when you need that crossroads for magic!

Anyway, after Djezèl had untied the crab's claws and freed it, he put four calabash bowls down, one at each corner of the crossroads.

In Bosou's room, in the temple, I had watched the ounsi fill the four bowls with the traditional Ginen food for Spirits: pieces of plantain, sweet potato, and pumpkin mixed with beans and corn kernels. There was a white candle stuck at the center of each bowl, as well as a few monben bata leaves, five red pennies, and a couple of odd feathers plucked from a red rooster.

Once the bowls were properly situated at the four corners and their candles lit, Djezèl dug a hole in the middle of the crossroads, ounsi singing Spirits-songs all the while.

He then had me stand in it, still stark naked except for my feet that were covered over by loose soil from the digging. Once again, he poured water over my head. He did not beat me with monben bata leaves this time. Instead, he scrubbed me with basil and other scented leaves and covered my entire body with a white powder. Then he told me to jump out of the hole both feet together. I did it perfectly.

This crossroads was truly deserted because no one, not a soul, passed by during the entire time we were there. The freed crab wasted no time in clearing out of our way, speeding sideways.

Afterwards, we walked to the cemetery closest to Djezèl's temple. It's a small country cemetery. We stood in front of Baron's cross.

Baron is Lord of the Dead. Baron's cross, in any cemetery, is always the first cross that's erected for the first burial.

I stood at the foot of the cross, asking for deliverance. My body was uncomfortably stiff.

"Baron Lacroix," I said, "I never gave anybody any problems. I never fought with anyone. Please let me feel new life. I need to breathe. Most of all, free me of Sasal, his wife, and of everyone pursuing me. I was born on November first, Day of the Dead, you know that, and that's how my sister gets to tease me all the time—she says Death would never take me because I am already dead. Maybe that's why I feel that life has passed me by. I have no life. Baron, give me my life back."

Sasal has been my good friend as far back as I can remember. We were part of a band. I played the guitar. Sasal was the band's treasurer. He never stole a cent. I knew I could always trust him. I didn't hesitate to help him when he told me about wanting to sell his land in the south. He promised that if I gave him a hand in getting the land ready—fence the whole property, put up a gate, register papers—he would halve the money with me when he sold it.

I didn't need to see the land or the deeds and I stood by him though everyone said "Watch out!" Especially my sister—she is always trying to make me feel small. I'd like to see her come back to live in Haiti now that our father, "her" Daddy, is dead, and make it in this country without his help.

Everybody is envious of everybody and people always hate even the smile on your face.

I gave Sasal every cent I could lay my hands on. It took him several years to fence the land and put up a gate. Then, Sasal found someone from the UN interested in the land but that man tried to get it for almost nothing. His name was John Brown. My sister set up several meetings with Sasal to go and meet John Brown. But Sasal is not the kind of man to put up with her power games so he never showed up. For months on end I gave Sasal all the money needed for paperwork to be done at lawyers, at the courthouse, at the mayor's offices, at the police and what not. That lasted for about two or three years.

Then, Sasal said he had another buyer and he needed more money for more papers, more lawyers, and the same things went on for another few years. But Sasal was tireless and never lost hope.

He did all the legwork while I did all the financing. We were brothers.

Or rather, I thought we were. I should have remembered the proverb: "Zanmi lwen se lajan sere, zanmi pre se kouto de bo"—A friend living far away is like gold in storage, while a friend close by is a double-edged knife.

I even borrowed money from my mother. She always complains

at first but she eventually gives in. Also, she is terrified of Sasal (like everyone else), because he is a Vodou priest too, like Djezèl. She figured that the sooner the deal was done the sooner Sasal would be out of my life.

She had heard from Venant that Sasal had gone to Les Cayes and sold my soul to a *bòkò*—a sorcerer—so he could do whatever he wanted with me. A Vodou priest takes care mostly of the worship of Spirits, even when they "work with both hands," but when a bòkò does magic, it's always evil.

My mother says she does not believe in Vodou but she fears it like hell on earth.

She refuses to admit that the world is so complicated it's OK to deal with it any way that works. She wants to pray to one God only. I tell her that in Vodou there is also one God, the Gran Mèt, and that Spirits do the same job Saints do; they are God's ambassadors.

"Nonsense!" she says. "It's only magic and a bunch of black sorcerers with black faces that frighten me. And when they wear dark glasses it's even worse. I don't want to hear anything about it."

That does not keep her from being very interested in my blue ring though . . . Well, she is French. She never got used to Haitian ways. Like all of us, she misses her own kind. The saying goes: "Chak bourik ranni nan patiraj li"—Every donkey hee-haws in its own pasture.

I succeeded in borrowing money from my sister only once. It was tough—she does not like to let go of her money. I tried a second time and lied about where the money was going. I said I needed to buy wood for a sculptor friend of mine who had a big order and who'd share his profits with me. When she found out the truth, she went to Sasal's to get it back. I don't know why I agreed to take her there. I also thought she'd chicken out on the way since everyone is so afraid of him. Sasal lived in the slums at the bottom of the ravine on the way to Canape Vert. That was their first meeting.

My sister wasn't prepared to like my friend and she didn't. But she did like Krikri, the white Pekingese dog. A Frenchman gave it to Sasal when he left Haiti.

There is a Gede Spirit at Sasal's who hates Krikri. "Where is that animal they call Krikri?" the Gede asks every time he comes down and possesses someone. "Krikri! Krikri! Come here! It's high time I eat you!" Krikri yelps, runs for cover, doesn't come out until the next morning.

But that day my sister first met Sasal, he did give her the money back. I was stunned. I don't like to borrow from either mother or sister; they feel self-righteous and see me as a kind of crook, just like Sasal. But I knew, in the end, that I would have the last laugh.

Sasal came to visit my mother a few times. He wanted to show his good faith and explain the situation. We borrowed from her then too. My mother is easy to charm.

Now, she is becoming more and more reclusive. She is afraid of everything. The watchman has strict orders not to let anyone in. Sasal's last visit to my mother didn't go so well. After that visit, I avoided crossing paths with him because I would have had to beat him up and I know my strength—I don't want to kill him.

What happened is that I had begun to doubt Sasal. I stopped giving him money. I told Djezèl how everyone is after my money since my father died.

Djezèl said to me then, "Your family's Spirits are neglected. It's well known your father followed African ways. He served Vodou Spirits. Look at all the trees your father planted on his land—he had the knowledge—each tree is a shrine."

Djezèl made sense. So I handed him a lot of money for a splendid feast to the Spirits. I started wearing the blue ring. Sasal was desperate.

MOTHER

I am French and I am proud of it. That's right. And I'll never understand anything about all this savagery I see going on here! Imagine: Sasal does magic spells on my son! "Wanga" they call it in this God-forsaken country! Wanga! Wanga! I have had it with their wanga! And this devil of a man goes so far as to sell my child's soul to some bòkò.

Dieu du ciel! God in Heaven! Where are you?

How is it that my Justin is so blind to what Sasal has been doing?! It's like there is a lid on his brain and a veil over his eyes. This is horrific magic and it's happening around us all the time! Even I! *Mon Dieu!* I believed in the land deal! On and off, yes, but, still, I believed. I also *wanted* to believe. I gave money for that land. *Seigneur!* I would have given anything to get this deal settled and that sorcerer out of Justin's life. Now I feel mortified.

Has anyone even *seen* this land?

I even went so far as to welcome Sasal in my house and he tried to explain the whole affair to me, his version of it.

He can be quite charming, mind you, but I cannot overlook the fact that he is an *oungan*—these Vodou priests are not to be trusted. I don't believe in Vodou and yet I am careful. I avoid it like the plague but it sticks to the very air one breathes. When it comes to Vodou, I am blue with fear. My daughter says that I react like a racist and that I speak like one too.

How can I not be afraid, the way I hear things in the night? Drums and drums and screams. Both the sky and I are livid.

I so wish that my children would stay away from all that. I regret ever coming to this God-forsaken place. I miss my father.

It must have taken some courage for Sasal to come here in spite of my dogs—most Haitians are terrified of dogs; people say it's colonial memory because of the way dogs were used against slaves.

I showed him my family albums—I can't help it, I always give people the benefit of the doubt and I give everyone a chance to redeem themselves. I shared memories of my family with Sasal and my photo albums are all that I have left of them. My childhood feels so far it is as if I dreamt it. The girl I was who looks at me from the paling photographs seems so sweet and trusting she breaks my heart. Sasal appeared very interested. I showed him my father on a horse in the Maisons-Laffite Park.

He commented on my father's long white hair brushed back and showing his high forehead. He looked at my blond mother wearing a white evening gown, standing by her piano. I told him about my dashing uncle Jacques who worked for Paramount in Paris and had bought Gary Cooper's car. I recounted how we spent the war days in a castle, how the old moldy maid who owned it fell in love with Jacques and, batting her eyelashes, invited him to sleep in the very canopy bed in which Liszt slept with Marie d'Agoult.

All this must have been very foreign to Sasal but I wanted him to respect my family and my son. Sasal was polite. I grant him that.

Now, no one comes here at all.

It's true I told the watchman not to let anyone in. Who is there to invite anyway? Everyone I loved is dead, my daughter lives in America, and Justin lives like a bum, even mingles with bums. *Dieu du ciel!* Things make him claustrophobic—he does not want to own anything except for that blue ring. He gives away everything he owns, even the shirt on his back. I know he feels for the poor but there must be a limit. He keeps his room locked. No one can go in. "Let the dust in my room rest in peace!" he yelled at me when I showed up with a mop and dust-cloth. "The dust is part of my things. The dust is mine. I am dust." Can you imagine what it's like for a mother to hear that?

No one needs me anymore, not even to play the maid.

But I don't give up. I never give up. You have to be a boxer with life. There is a bed in Justin's room now. At least I know my son has a bed and he is not like some barefoot vagabond with not even a mattress of his own.

"May I store it here?" I asked him. "It's not yours. You can't sell or give it away but you can use it if you want." Dear me! The things a mother has to do. He was not fooled. Nevertheless, he let me in.

One thing he loves is our land. Things will have to be different when we sell it. God only knows what will happen to us.

Everybody is scared of Sasal and I am not ready to forget his last visit to me. He came with that wife of his. His consort under the devil's care! The watchman's heart must have jumped to his throat when he saw these two show up. Just imagine the sight: Sasal wearing all black, cracking a whip every few steps, and his wife, a frog look-alike, wearing all red.

Our idiot watchman hid behind a bush and let the pair cross the "whole nine yards" from the street gate down to my own gate that unfortunately was open just then. The dogs were inside with me, and it must be the whip they heard that got them barking because when I peered down from my window I saw Black and Red looking right at me, whip cracking.

"What do you want?" I asked. Imagine my fright! The devil himself had gotten in. *Dieu du ciel!*

My friend Mrs. Selas, whose husband is a big-time lawyer, said I should have challenged Sasal and the red frog. They did not have any proof on the claim they came to make but my old heart was beating so fast I couldn't think and I would have done anything to get them out of my land even if it meant signing any paper they handed me or escorting them out personally in my own car. And I did both these things, I must admit.

"You need to scare Sasal," Mrs. Selas said. "Just make a date with him, promise you will give him what he wants, and then pay off some husky policemen to show up at the appointment. But, most of all, have a camera ready. I'll lend you my Polaroid. Because if there is something these people really fear, it is to have their pictures taken."

I told Mrs. Selas that I did what I did because Sasal had gotten ahold of Justin's passport and you can't fool around with someone who's got your passport. "How the hell did he get Justin's passport?" she asked. I told her I did not know—how could I tell her that Justin himself gave it to him for safekeeping?

SASAL

"I want my money!" That's what I told the old hag.

These bourgeois, they all the same: big walls like they can have an island just for themselves, big gates, big land, big cars, big dogs, big pretensions. I'm not impressed.

I'm not scared of their watchmen or their dogs. Their dogs are an image of their own faces. When they need you they open all the doors. When they don't need you they don't know you.

"What do you want?" she yelled—like I am some shit smelling up her front door.

"I want my money!"

When she thought I could do something for her son she was all welcome—it was "How do you dooo . . . ?" Then drinks and food bits and family photos. Freaks in frills, that's what they are. Now the cemetery isn't good enough for them either—they've got the old man buried on his land, in his garden, and under his favorite tree! At least he is underground now, he won't be kicking the poor off it anymore.

Nobody is supposed to come near her. Like she's too good to even talk to you. You ask for her at the gate, they tell you she's not there. You call on the phone, she hang up on you. You ask for Justin, she hang up on you. You come to see Justin and they tell you he left since morning. You wait for him all day under the sun knowing full well he's hiding inside until you leave. Finally you leave because you know you have some face left of your own and you're not going to hand that over to them too.

But coming to my place, Justin feels that's his right. *They* all do. And *they* won't even bother to come personally sometimes— just send some go-getter and, "Tell Sasal I want to see him." Like that sister of his did last time she was here. When Justin want to see Sasal, it's easy to find Sasal—it's down the ravine in the slums. He come in without knocking because there's no gate, no ghoul, no growling dog—Krikri wagged her tail, she think he live here—one gray mud shack like all the other gray mud shacks. Except mine has a red flag floating above the tin roof—yes, I am an oungan. And he like that, Justin—he like it when everybody's afraid of his friend. He like it that his family, and even the old lady, is scared of his friend. His friend got no money but he got power that money can't buy, power that can do things to you. He don't want to harm you, Justin, but he like to scare you. For him Vodou isn't real religion—just stuff to make scarecrows. He's like that, Justin—likes power.

Never mind we're old buddies. Because he wasn't always like that, Justin. That's what I liked about him—a good heart, always listens to you, no one is below him, a good Christian, faith healer, his pockets always empty because he gave it all to anyone who asked for help on his way. That's why his old man gave him so little—just handed him pocket money, like a kid. Bourgeois don't like to share even with their own. No matter though, Justin helped me out a lot. That's why I made him the offer about the land my uncle in Les Cayes left me. I wanted to do something for Justin too. We were equals in misery. We were brothers.

I ended up busting my ass for years about that land. Justin didn't have to do nothing. I am the one who hustled after buyers and ran after all sorts of documents they kept asking for. None of that rains on you like ripe mangoes do. But *they're* finding out how hard it is to sell land.

Justin is like a madman since his old man died. That's when he started turning on me. Like he's trying to turn into the old man. I don't care. I never went to that damn house of theirs when the old man was alive anyway. I didn't need to give him my face to kick like some street dog. The way the old man acted you'd think some dead man's soul was fumbling in his brain. Good thing he didn't like dogs—if he had any then he would've sent them after you.

I only went there after the old man died. Justin wasn't coming around here so much except when he needed us to do something for him. Bourgeois can never take care of their own needs. They got to have slaves running around doing work for them. Bitches, Dominicans looking for tricks, street bums—everybody was after Justin's new money now. I tried to warn him but he wasn't listening no more. I tried to talk to the old lady but, like I told you, she hang up on me. And that sister of his guard the place like it's all hers. I told Justin he should watch out with her. But I don't have time to worry about him. I am a poor man. I have my wife, my children, and my children's mothers to take care of. I take any job I find.

I should've known Justin wasn't gonna give us the money back. He said he'd pay us in a month. I told my wife, "Cocotte, Justin has been coming and going at my house for I don't know how many years now. You cook his food. You wash his clothes. But I don't like what I see happening—Justin's been going to Djezèl. That man now control Justin's head."

But Cocotte knew Justin for all these years. She tell me, "Justin need it for a good cause. I'll borrow from my sister. He can give us his passport as guarantee." Soon as Justin get the money, he don't come around at all. Even in the street I never bump into him.

My wife's sister's going crazy. She need her money to buy stuff in Santo Domingo she resell here for good money. So I go to Djezèl's to check things out, see if I learn anything. I find Justin there, sitting in front of a pile of money and wearing a new blue ring. "Oh! Justin giving out freebies," I said. "I'm taking my share." It's not until I got home I counted the bills. And that's when I said to my wife, "Cocotte, we're going to the old lady's." We got justice over there and from the old lady the paper to prove it. Afterwards, we even went to surprise-visit that sister too. I am not afraid of her. I told her about Djezèl. "D'you know," I says to her, "what else was on the table next to that pile of money? Your photo. Yes ma'am. His own sister. He was giving Djezèl more money on top of what he already borrow from us." And I told her more stuff. Like what it is Djezèl was going to do with the money and why Justin wanted that done. I gave her a big shock. It's hard to tell though—that sister, you never know what she's thinking.

SISTER

I had left the house in a huff with the bewildered rooster tucked under my arm. I sat him unceremoniously in my car on the seat next to mine and drove off. I was passing through the Place du Champs de Mars when I suddenly came upon a crowd that was blocking the street. The rooster stretched its plucked, bony neck and red-crested head up to the open window and screamed.

A traveling circus was in town. They had come from a South American country and were presently showing off some of the animals by walking through the main streets of downtown Port-au-Prince. Tigers, elephants, and an odd assortment of other wild animals were visiting Haiti.

It might have been the heat that got to the rooster's head but the crowd must have taken it as an alarm signal or something of a threat because they shifted their whole attention from the circus animals to concentrate on the scream that came from my car.

No one in the crowd appeared to find it strange that I'd be driving around town with a rooster as my only company. Instead, people reacted in silent unison and parted themselves to let me go

through on what they must have thought was a special mission—
why else would a woman in Haiti be driving past the presidential
palace at almost midday with an untied rooster propped up on the
seat next to hers?

Everybody knows that a red rooster is both the emblem of the
president's political party and also of Papa Ogou, the Vodou war-
rior Spirit who many believe led the slaves' insurrection against
the French. They wanted to free themselves and free the land.
Ha! Who is ever free? You free yourself of something only to
quickly fall prey to something else. "Cut heads! Burn houses!"
was Déssalines's battle cry. He was a fierce leader, an imposing
black man who hated the French. The way I was feeling that day,
it was this rooster's head I might have cut off.

My battle with it had begun several days before, along with my
battle with Sasal.

"Who owns that screaming cock that has been keeping
me up all night for a week?" I asked the night watchman one
morning.

"It's for Ivnè, the new gardener."

"Why is the cock in my garden and not at Ivnè's?"

"Maybe he wants to keep an eye on it."

"Why?"

"It's a fighting cock. All his money's in this cock."

"I am telling you, and you tell Ivnè—any cock I hear or find on
my land, it's mine."

Three days later I was still hearing the rooster every night.
It starts up at one P.M. and goes on every hour on the hour, increasing its pitch. I heard it coming from different angles of the
garden—I concluded there was more than one.

"There are two cocks in my yard," I told the night watchman at
the crack of dawn. "Whose are they?"

"I told Ivnè to take his cock out of here the same day you told
me to."

"It's still here and it's not alone. Whose is the other one?"

"Maybe it's mine."

"You have one too! How come you only remembered Ivnè's
when I asked you?"

"Mine don't have his voice yet."

"Well, he does now. And I never heard of a voiceless cock."

The next morning, the day I bumped into the circus, I was inspecting the upkeep of the land and happened to look into the toolshed. I found a red rooster tied to a shovel. Standing close by under a tamarind tree, I noticed Ivnè watching me. I called him to come closer. "Whose cock is this?" I asked.

"That one is Lola's—the watchman's daughter."

"Not any more," I said. "Now, it's mine."

I untied the rooster and tucked it under my arm. I sent for the watchman. He came quickly and looked sheepish.

"Whose cock is this?" I asked him.

"I thought Ivnè took it home already."

"Ivnè says it belongs to Lola."

"It *was* hers. But she sold it to Ivnè. He said he'd take it home."

Hearing the watchman's voice, the rooster blasted his.

"He recognizes me," the watchman said, and smiled, visibly moved.

"Is this the cock with no voice yet?"

"Yes."

"This cock is yours then?"

"No. It's Ivnè's."

In the thirty minutes that had elapsed since I had gotten the rooster from the shed and tied it to a chair at the house, it had three shits, five blasting screams, had refused water, and kept its head ensconced in its shoulders. I asked to speak with Lola. She came quickly.

"Lola, whose cock is this?"

"Ivnè's."

"Ivnè says it's yours."

"I sold it to him. I thought he took it home already."

"How can you say you thought Ivnè had taken it home? You live here with your father. You hear that cock as well as I do—you know it is here and not at Ivnè's. Anyway, Ivnè says the cock is yours. Why does he say that?"

"He hasn't paid me yet."

"Then how can he take it home if it's not his yet?"

"Ivnè knows I sold him the cock because it could not stay here. He had to take it home. Even before he could pay me."

"'Was going to,' 'had to,' 'sold,' 'not sold'! I am sick of your stories! This cock that 'has no voice' is not yours, not your father's, not Ivnè's. It's mine!"

I stuck the rooster in the car with me so I could have time to think of what to do with it next. I had to leave in a rush for an appointment with a lawyer downtown. I needed legal advice about Sasal. I was going to the same lawyer who had advised me on issues around property ownership. Since my father's death, I had been trying to sell our land. The rooster could have been comic relief but I felt besieged. I saw both Sasal and that silly bird as inopportune invaders.

Two days before, Venant had given me a long speech: "I know Sasal ever since he is a kid, and ever since I been working for your family," Venant said. "He can't be trusted—a thief, that's all he is; always been; always will be. That's all he knows. That's all he cares to know. I warn you, your brother's soul's been sold. Sure as my name is Venant, your brother's been sold. You need a good oungan—fight back! My daughter can take you to one in Leogane. My legs hurt; otherwise, I'd take you there myself. I know everybody over there. Family picks up after family and so you should take care of saving your brother. Year after year I watch Justin going like a madman after money to give to Sasal! No. I can't take it any more. He wasn't like that before—Justin was sweet, went to prayer meetings, always had time for people. Look at his eyes now; they're empty."

I tried to shrug Venant's words off but I was shaken. I was not part of that world. How to function in it?

"Have you even *seen*," I asked Justin, "that Great Wall of China you are building around Sasal's land? Do you get receipts for all the money you give? If that land exists and if it sells, will the half you get still be worth more than all the money you have been giving Sasal for the past . . . what? Fifteen years? Have you ever been to the national archives, the mayor's office, the tax-collection offices, lawyers, police department, all the public or private offices Sasal claimed he needed papers from, and for which you endlessly forked out endless amounts? Have you ever met the Baptist Church buyers? The UN buyer? What was his name again?"

"John Brown."

"John Brown? Like the street we live on?"

"Yes."

One time, years ago, I paid a visit to Sasal with Justin who walked in without knocking. Sasal had a snake's hypnotic grace, a feminine voice that spoke in a hush, pale green eyes that in contrast to his black skin appeared without color.

We sat in a clean, windowless room that had a bed in one corner. Through the embrasure which was missing a door, I could see the turquoise color of the adjoining room whose walls were covered with life-size representations of Vodou Spirits: Bosou Twa Kòn looked like a snarling, knife-brandishing, red-eared, plump devil with three horns; an image of Saint Sebastian was pinned up under his left elbow; Èzili Dantò, eyes bulging and fixed on me, was framed with images of the Black Madonna, the Immaculate Conception, Saint George, and Saint James. A long-haired angel held a pointed dagger. An altar was draped with gold Christmas banderoles. A cross, planted in the ground, had a necklace made from various bits of bones wrapped around its top. Nailed low in a corner, a shiny tapestry showed Christ with the apostles sitting at the holy table; there Judas stood, pointing at Christ with both hands.

That was then. Now, downtown Port-au-Prince, circus animals had crossed paths with a rooster.

Soon afterwards, I made a date to meet Sasal again because he had begun to harass my mother. It had been over ten years since I had seen him last. Whenever I was in Haiti, Sasal stayed away from the house. I knew he was coming and going freely with Justin as soon as I left.

I knew Justin would not show up for that new meeting with Sasal. He always eclipsed himself as much as possible and would now especially, since, because of him, Sasal had been able to come frighten and force my mother into making a deal.

Nothing was really unusual in Justin's behavior except for a ring with a blue stone he was now wearing. Judging by his grin and evasiveness when he was asked about the ring, it became clear to me that the ring was unclear and that its assumed power was clear.

Noticing that I was looking at his ring, Justin whispered to me,

"I know an oungan, Djezèl, he works for all the rich people in the neighborhood. He handles their problems."

"Do they all wear blue rings?" I whispered back.

I felt desolate and remembered my father, the man who missed mass said in Latin and who cried to organ music, the lover of French gardens, French wives, and General de Gaulle.

I could still hear the "Ave Maria" we played for his funeral and that he loved partly because Maria was his mother's name. I also remembered Pauline, the grandmother my mother loved more than her own mother and who taught me that a lady's nails should always be polished; Pauline, born in Les Cayes, a dusty town in the south of Haiti, from Frenchmen who had fled France when Frenchmen were slaughtering Frenchmen because Frenchmen wanted their land free of aristocrats; Pauline who married a Frenchman at fifteen, never saw Haiti again, never missed Haiti, nor its people, because they were black people who had slaughtered Frenchmen because they wanted their land free of white colonialists.

In Haiti, land is still an issue we handle our way.

My friend Max told me about his niece's husband who had problems with squatters: a *tonton macoute* police had moved in on his property with his whole family. The husband hired someone strong with police connections; that "someone" showed up on the land at dawn with a truckload of paid-off policemen in uniforms who were shooting rifles in the air.

The hired man drove the truck right to the macoute's front door; he dropped an empty black coffin marked with a painted white cross and skull and warned, "If you're still here tomorrow, this coffin is gonna be yours."

Sasal had now succeeded in holding my father's once-lovely French bride at the throat.

Dressed all in black, Sasal stood with his wife dressed all in red at my mother's door. This was gut-level theater. "Justin owes me money," Sasal shouted. "He didn't sign any paper about it but he gave me his passport to hold. I want justice. I want it any way I can get it. I want my money." His wife was cracking her whip like a punctuation mark for her husband's speech. My mother felt faint.

Never mind that Justin had been in the habit of storing his

belongings at Sasal's—clothes, papers, and all—instead of using his own room. Never mind also that he had been supporting Sasal and his family all these years, either with direct gifts of money or indirect ones through the pretense of the land preparation and sale.

My mother signed a paper saying she'd pay Justin's debt in several Monday installments. Having done this, she acknowledged the debt and bound us all to Sasal.

By the time I came home from the U.S., my mother had already paid Sasal two of the installments.

The first Monday after my arrival in Haiti, Sasal did not show up for his third installment.

The second Monday, still no Sasal.

By the third, he calls my mother. Fortunately, I answered the phone.

I told him that my mother has reached an age when she deserves her peace, that I was not leaving Haiti knowing she'll get harassed every Monday, that from now on, the only dog at the gate he'll deal with is me.

Ivnè got his cock back. It took the rooster only one fight in the arena for Ivnè to be able to pay Lola—that rooster not only had a voice but he had a bloodletting beak, killer claws, an assassin's drive.

I was talking to Ivnè when Sasal, a few days after our phone conversation, showed up unexpectedly with Cocotte.

I would not have recognized Sasal if Ivnè had not been gesticulating excitedly behind his back and pointing to him nervously until I understood what he was doing. The snake was now a bloated iguana. Cocotte was a plump woman who talked too much.

She told me how Justin had worked out a special deal with Djezèl to keep me from selling the family land. "You'll be reimbursing us," she said with a snarl, "money Justin borrowed so he could pay to sell your soul."

River
Valley
Rooms

THE GATE

If I were to tell about Justin in a kind of present-day diary that also takes glimpses of the past, I would start with the time when he stood near the gate with his new green felt hat on. A grown man, he looked as if he were about to go out on business or just came back from it.

But Justin is not going anywhere.

It's the look that he liked. It had the color of the cap our father wore when he was building winding stairways and rental apartments throughout our garden property. Yet, Justin's hat was too small for his head and had a narrow rim not efficient against the

Caribbean sun overhead. It was more like those worn by judges who rule in our Haitian provincial courts of law and travel on donkeys from one small town to another.

The green hat sat on top of Justin's head—funny, sweet, odd, misplaced, inefficient, childlike, and vulnerable to the wind.

Before the gate was built, our property was a passageway for all those who had business coming here as well as for those who had none.

Of those who had no business being here, some crossed through the garden to get to the river slums at the bottom edge of it where they live; others were an assortment of beggars, street-girls, jobless men, and con men who came after Justin for money—they either wanted charity or to strike a deal. Justin loves to do both, even if it means using up his weekly allowance or having to borrow from anyone, even me.

Justin needs to feel he is some sort of businessman because that's what our father had hoped he could be, like the men in our family are now and have been for generations.

It seems to hardly matter to Justin that he gets fooled. His pride and power is not in having success but in participation. Early on in our childhood, it had been clear that his natural gifts were laid outside of logic and the practical world.

The neighborhood's poor children also came to the garden. They sneaked in for water and filled up plastic buckets to bring back home to their mothers. For these children, the new white gate turned out to be a blessing, even if at first it seemed otherwise—when old Judge Labrosse, Justin's friend who rented one of the apartments, realized that the children were not allowed to get through the wrought iron gate, he decided to invite them for daily milk and snacks; from water thieves, the children were turned into afternoon guests.

They came in a cluster, empty buckets in hand. When the watchman opened the gate, they pushed in like sheep rushing out of the barn, hurrying past the white gate with shrieks of joy and eyes twitching from the intensity of sudden light over a wealthy place. The children looked dazed from the vastness of the garden and the whiteness of the great house—these were children growing in the darkness of shacks as if they were an artificially created breed made unusually resistant and oblivious to being cramped, to oppressive heat, airlessness, hunger and foul-smelling trash.

There is a photograph of Justin standing at the entrance of the property before the gate was built. Ten years old and eating a *kenèp* fruit, he casts me a suspicious glance as I snatch his photo. He gnawed like a rodent at the round seed's peach-colored, meager flesh.

There is a vast array of ways in which Justin has looked at me. For instance, I remember his eyes when our father would ask me to join him for a stroll in the garden. I felt his eyes from a distance while Father and I walked. Justin was never asked for a walk.

The gate, however, is an illusion. You come to it down a short alleyway. It is held between two freestanding stone pillars around which there is enough space for people to easily squeeze through.

But the illusion is commonly agreed upon and generally holds— people stand at the gate and wait for the watchman to unlock the padlock, loosen the heavy chain, and open.

Nowadays, Jean is watchman at the gate. I gave him drawing paper pads and a box of color pencils to occupy himself with in between openings and closings. He draws black chicken after black chicken on every page. Each time he opens the gate for me, he brings me his most recent drawing to admire. All of Jean's chickens have his grin.

LETTER TO MY LATE FATHER

Dear Father, there are letters that I write to you every day but only in my mind because paper and stamped envelopes no longer can reach you.

I want to say that Justin misses you.

He still stands at the gate, like he always did, as if he knew you would one day die right there; as if he knew something that would change his life forever would happen right there; that if he kept standing watch he might be present when it was happening and be able to prevent it; that he might even stop your little green truck that came speeding down the alley, out of control, with you having fainted at the wheel, and keep it from crashing on a lamppost.

He stood at the gate as if he knew he would be needed to pull you out of the car, your chest heaving; try a mouth-to-mouth resuscitation he never learnt.

Your shoes, Father, now on my feet, feel too big and look bleak.

You have left me a lush but rotting world to manage—inheriting this land and all you built on it.

This place is its own country.

Apartments we rent form a miniature city with its ongoing generations of tenants who create a kind of history both generated and held by walls that repeatedly need to be patched up, repaired, covered up so they can stop crumbling and continue to hold this din I hear from everyone's psyche until they start foaming again with saltpeter as if they were the very sweating, aging, and ailing skin of those people they time and again shield, shelter, and constrict.

The money you left us has begun to suffocate the air between people and me.

I used to idle kindly like the flame of a candle. Coconut trees were like bursts of wings on the light lemon page of the dawn sky. Clouds were special friends I made while I dreamt of my childhood.

I collected stories from illiterate people who liked telling them and seeing the designs I made on paper with things they said to me. The orderly progression of words I wrote reflected their wish to see direction and form in their lives. Words on the page gave each person a strange, individual face and brought them out of invisible abstraction.

But now, since the day you died, I sit next to an accountant. I write payrolls. My hair is cut short. I bargain.

In the bedroom I occupy, I stand on a round, woven straw rug that has a design in which smaller circles cluster and constellate around a larger center.

I close the wood shutters and pull the curtains. There is a peace in their whiteness that invites sleep.

Rain pours like a woman overcome with the need to tell.

Trees you planted stand taller now already than when you knew them. They watch me like the hermetic dead, dark and dense against the gray glow of the evening.

I light a votive candle. The flame shivers. Santa Clara's figure is poised in blue on the candle's transparent glass. Silence is a blanket. Sound from a fallen fruit becomes company. A wide empty chair stands in a corner of my room.

Here, there are walls within walls.

DAUGHTERS

Each morning when I wake, my heart feels locked at a gate.

I hear the calls of chicks that gather and whirl around their mother in a moving imitation of my bedroom rug's design. She seems their only thought. She shows them a feathered dance in which she scratches the ground, pecks, backs up, scratches, pecks, goes forward, scratches, pecks . . . Dry leaves that surround them are like the crumpled paper on which God discards His thoughts.

I read somewhere that sorrow is what differentiates human beings from animals, that only those who have a soul can know sorrow because they are capable of thoughts about their thoughts.

I watch. I listen. The lanky, sun-deprived papaya plant below my window over the pool has managed to bear a tiny green fruit that huddles all the way at the top among sparse leaves that spread lacy, green fingers out of their flat palms. But this fruit is what here is called *ròròt*—it will never ripen to any fullness. Justin noticed it too and often stops by. He watches it in silence.

The papaya plant has the Byzantine tallness of the wooden Madonna on my desk and on whose bosom an infant Christ seems to have climbed to clutch her veil. On this sculpture, the face of Saint Anne's daughter looks amused and tender.

Daughters are the caress on the cheek, a gentle breeze that curls inside a vessel and waits to gather. They nestle jewels on their necks and ears and smile their mothers' smiles.

Their lives are the interlocking of moments they preserve in photo albums. They treasure their grandmothers' dishware, bake sweet breads, and with the pink tea they boil from red hibiscus they relieve you from the hurt of colds. They paint their mothers' aged toenails and, almost out of compassion, eventually develop the same curved backs.

Lines in their hands record all the feelings that rose from those they have touched. Their eyes are the screens on which the family stories are projected. Daughters contain.

JUDGE LABROSSE'S PATIO

Judge Labrosse had been appointed president of the Haitian Supreme Court. He would therefore be president if anything happened to the president.

He was stone deaf.

He appeared more useful sitting on his patio than at court. There, he maintained a unique peace and profound courtesy toward all. Justin sat among the children each afternoon, competing for milk and cookies.

Once the children and Justin had left, the Judge took a walk in the garden. He held a stick with which he poked at fallen leaves, mumbling all the while, and then impatiently struck them out of his path.

The Judge's apartment was a sectioned off part of the main house that had been my parents' before their divorce.

After his divorce from my mother, and prior to the coming of the Judge, my father lived in that apartment. The bedroom was a long, low-ceiling, windowless, air-conditioned space. My father called it "the tomb" but didn't die there. He spent interminable nights of depression in this room until he remarried a woman who had the same name as my mother.

In later years, the Judge died there.

My father introduced me to his fiancée in what became the patio where the Judge would entertain children from the slums. That day, I sat on a red-cushioned chair and remembered the American man who had also lived in that house when I was a child. Each afternoon, after coming home from work at the mattress factory he owned, this gentle old man treated me to crackers and cheese cut in small cubes while he sipped rum cocktails and observed me; his eyes were a warm hue of blue; I nibbled the cheese bits shyly and speedily and he said that I was a pretty-pretty little mouse.

My father's fiancée came out of my father's tomb wearing a black dress. He warned her that she and I could never be friends.

Being deaf, the Judge spoke too loud and everything he said while sitting on his patio could be heard from a good distance away. His hearing aid was forever being repaired and he was forever expecting some new one.

"I will take you to Zaire with me," he said to Justin. "I live in exile from there because of Monboutou."

"Yes," answered Justin with a different glow in his eyes.

"When I was there, I never felt that I was in exile from here even though Haiti is my birth country. I made lots of money. There is lots of gold there and I have many friends."

When the Judge's brother visited from their childhood town in the hills behind Gonaïves, I found that he spoke louder than the Judge did. He was not deaf but he too wanted to be heard.

Justin would often leave the Judge's patio with a full pack of his favorite cookies. He held them close to his heart like his dreams of Zaire.

Judge Labrosse died in his sleep. Benicia, his maid, was used to sleeping on a floor mattress at the foot of his bed. One morning she got up and found him lifeless. It was dawn, the time when Semi, the Judge's cat, came back from his night of harassing rats.

On the day of the Judge's funeral, my mother hosted his family in the lobby of our old house. He had no children. A sister we never knew came from Canada and the brother we knew came from the hills behind Gonaïves. Nieces and nephews were there to settle scores and everybody wanted money. The sister from Canada wanted her share while the brother from Gonaïves thought she did not deserve any. The Judge had no money anyway. He fled Zaire without the money in his bank account and he never stopped dreaming about his gold rush back to Zaire.

When the family left, bitterness had been reaffirmed. Benicia put Semi in a bag and took him away.

JEAN

Nowadays, Justin buys his own cookies. At the gate, he sits with Jean and offers him some.

Jean stands guard at the gate.

But, come November first—All Souls' Day—his mind visibly tilts off balance. Come November second—All Saints' Day—Jean tells you, "I am not the one you know. I am all Spirit. What the Spirits want is what I want. What I do is what they remember. My body is of the wind."

When Jean speaks like this, I know the gate is ajar.

BETTY'S ROOM

On a recent night, I opened my apartment door to take the trash out. A tarantula moved out of a corner. I let out a cry, dropped the trash, shut the door.

I attract tarantulas.

My mother says that after finding one by my head in my crib, she always kept the crib covered with a mosquito net. Jean assures me that tarantulas belong to the Spirits of the Dead.

In the old house, I had a pink bathroom. A tarantula lived there. I made a pact with it.

"If you don't move, I don't move," I said.

One night, I bashed it with a broom. It curled itself and shrank into something black and insignificant as it died. That death still worries my conscience even though it had moved first. Since then, the same spider keeps turning up in my life.

It showed up again tonight.

I live in the same apartment in which Betty lived. Each night, I stand in her bedroom and pull the curtains before going to sleep.

Gigi, Betty's cat, had lost so much of her fur that when I patted her back I called her Sweetie Rat. Alan did not like it when I teased his mother's cat. Gigi had the same minced chicken breast dinner every night. I suggested that she should be given a rat or allowed to get one for herself. Alan said that she was not allowed out, and if I continued making fun of Gigi I would not be allowed in.

Gigi waited all day to have dinner with Betty in front of the TV. Both sat on the bed with a tray in front of them.

Alan preferred to watch stars outside with me.

He ate his dinner quickly so he could meet with me and Betty resented it. He always hoped for a shooting star that would give him the chance of a wish.

I disliked watching stars when I was a child.

I sat with my parents on the green bench that was on the terrace above the pool. The sadness in my mother prevented me from seeing the stars. My father loved quiet. My mother's sorrows felt noisy. After my father left for work in the morning, she played music very loud throughout the house.

Both my parents loved Betty. They saw her as a charming American who had elegance and wit. Betty's mother had died young and her older sister raised her. She often told me about her life when we sat together by the pool on Sunday afternoons. Once, she dipped her legs in the water and said, "Ooh . . . I had such beautiful legs . . ."

Alan was the friend I loved most. He lived with Gigi and Betty. Gigi couldn't wait for Betty to come home from work in the evening. Alan couldn't wait for her to leave for work in the morning. Alan showed me gay porno movies in Betty's bedroom while Gigi kept crossing the room with an offended look, back and forth, her rat tail lifted stiff and high like a menacing whip.

The tarantula showed up tonight because I had Betty's old room worked over in the morning. Hired workers pulled off the old plywood boards that had been nailed to the walls in the days when Betty lived there. It had been done at her request to cover up the saltpeter that kept foaming up. No matter how much saltpeter was scraped and freshly painted over, the walls bubbled up, cracked, and peeled open like unforgiving old wounds.

Today I saw that the plywood itself had rotted from the inside. It peeled off like skin and revealed walls that had never healed. Termites had created tunnels that linked isolated saltpeter sores to each other.

Gigi died in this room.

She was ill and in great pain. Betty called a vet. She wanted Gigi to be given a merciful shot. The vet came with a long and thick hypodermic needle. He made several attempts to insert it into Gigi's brittle, hairless spine. Gigi cried out each time. Betty too cried each time she heard Gigi's spine crack under the needle.

In the days of Gigi's life, Jean was a young man who sang Vodou songs to children and told them stories.

We are both middle-aged now and single. Unlike me, he has many children. They are scattered around the country, born from different mothers who all curse him because he sends no money to care for the children. He is no different from the men he grew up with.

Through the years, he has lost his teeth one by one. He is pleased with his new dentures that have a line of real gold showing between the upper front teeth. He got these new teeth when he lived with me in the Kenskoff Mountains and worked as my cook and housekeeper.

He spent his days climbing to neighboring fields looking for fresh vegetables for our evening meals together. He wore a long black winter coat I bought for him from a man who dealt second-hand clothes sent to Haiti as charitable donations from Canadian organizations. He sang while he cooked, different songs for different dishes. He liked fresh beans most.

CATS

Soulouque and Ramses were my cats. I took them to Kenskoff with me.

I thought that I would escape the voices from the walls if I left the valley. Nights in the mountains were chilly and the cats huddled with me on the bed. They roamed the mountain and when they returned in the evening their fur smelled of herbs. Soon, both were stolen—meat is rare at the dinner table of the poor. First, it was Soulouque.

Jean cried. "Soulouque was family," he said, tears running down his cheeks.

Ramses had a litter of four when she too disappeared, her nipples still pink and heavy with milk. Jean nursed the kitten with a baby bottle from a doll's set I bought downtown. O Chi Min was the kitten I kept.

She never was a trusting pet but she was loyal. She hunted and brought live lizards home as offerings to me. She exhausted them in a hopeless chase around the rooms until they died, and then laid their motionless, mauled bodies at my feet. She got upset at my frowning and would take them away. She jumped out the window with the dead lizard hung limp between her jaws. She taught mistrust to her own kitten and how never to get caught.

Justin liked Egyptian mythology. He named his son Ramses.

He admired pharaohs who had full control over their lives, even over the afterlife, and over others who saw them as gods, men and women willing to be walled in and die with them in the tomb, to accompany and serve them for eternity. Justin said that pharaohs' minds soared higher than eagles and that jewels adorning their breast held stones endowed with magical powers.

He saw each pharaoh as a meaningful link in a long dynasty of glorious men, revered and respected in their time and throughout history. He envied a son who could take over his father's crown and scepter.

But Justin's Ramses died of diarrhea within two months of his birth. I was abroad.

My father never knew he once had a grandson.

No one had dared tell my father about the birth of this child—he had never accepted Justin's marriage to a young black prostitute and had refused to meet her. My mother had not welcomed the girl happily but had accepted facts she could not change. She always keeps a protective eye on Justin, wherever he goes, whatever he does. But she said that Ramses was not Justin's son—he was too black and the mother was a prostitute.

Alone, Justin buried his child in the lower part of the garden, on a little grassy plateau he likes and from which you can hear the water of the river as it runs.

I don't know exactly when Justin started sleeping under the trees of this plateau. He said that he could not sleep indoors anymore—the rooms had no air and he had nightmares.

When he was a child, he had visions: he complained about being frightened by animals he saw under his bed. Doctors said there were abnormal pressures in his brain and gave him pills. Father took the news hard and treated Justin harshly thereafter, claiming he would make a man out of him.

Father suffered from depression the last twenty-five years of his life. There was a particularly difficult phase when he suffered anxiety attacks every night. He pleaded with me to watch over him and sleep by his bed. I refused.

Justin offered to do it. He unrolled his thin mattress over the rug at the foot of the big bed. When Father was anguished, he let his hand drop outside the bed. Justin held the hand that hung loose above him and spoke softly to soothe his father. This went on for a long time. Justin was happy. Father got better.

Afterward, Justin went back to sleeping under trees and avoiding his father. They met only when Justin was invited for lunch. When there was cake in the refrigerator, Father was careful not to leave Justin alone in the kitchen.

ALAN

A septic tank is not just one big hole into which excrements are flushed until it gets so full another hole needs to be dug up. It is actually divided into three sections and each one is lined with gravel at the bottom. Waste and liquids are filtered from one section to the other. What eventually gets to the third section is clear, odorless liquid. Matter stays in the first section where it does not pile up because it generates a kind of life-form that in turn feeds on it and keeps it leveled low. Open up the septic tank and they die from the light and fresh air—life necessities for these creatures are darkness and excrement.

In my mind's eye I see a lime-green bird, an acrobat. He flutters along up a thin branch until he reaches the very tip-end. Once there, he lets himself hang upside down. He holds on with small claws and balances in the breeze: "See what I can do?" That's the bird's game. It is a playful bird, the kind that, no matter what, never dies in the story or in your heart.

Among all the trees in the valley, Alan favored one tall, slim breadfruit tree that had managed to squeeze itself in between dense, great trees and reach for the sky.

Under Alan's feet, right where he liked to stand, was a septic tank, but he did not know it.

"I can fly," he'd say. "Really, I can. You don't believe me. You think me a fool filled with fantasy. But I know it's only fear that holds me back. I need only to open my arms wide and let myself drop in space. I know I cannot fall. I will soar above trees. I'll follow the river all the way to the sea. You could come with me."

"Jump," I'd say, "or light up that joint."

"Tough broad," he'd say and chuckle.

He had a dimple on his left cheek. My own dimple is on the right. I see him as he always was, wearing the white kimono I gave him that took on colors from the moon. The kimono reached almost to his ankles. He put it on every night after dinner and went out to the garden to look at the stars.

There was a spot he liked best because trees had not yet blocked the view to Port-au-Prince Bay. I imagine him as he claimed he could be seen—flying over the mountains of my childhood, kimono sleeves flapping and upholding him as wings would; no matter how far he flies, he always turns around so I can see the dimple near his smile, moon-etched. And I shout to him, "Strange birds flying these days!"

I had met Alan once when I came home alone for a short vacation. We bumped into each other in the stairway of an apartment building.

"Oh, bonjou Matmwazèl . . ." he said in Kreyòl while leaning on the stair rail. "Care for a cigarette?"

"No," I said, "I don't smoke . . . cigarettes."

"Ooh . . . I see . . . Come then, we'll try something else."

He invited me over to his room. We were friends from then on.

"Don't waste your charm on that handsome one with the green eyes," my mother said to me the next day after we had bumped into him. "He was a New York fashion model . . . pretty boy . . . if you see what I mean?"

By the time Alan and I met, he had become a wigs merchant. He bought blond and red wigs and hairpieces in Miami and sold them to street vendors in downtown Port-au-Prince. They called him Monsieur Alan.

He was Justin's only friend before Judge Labrosse came to live in the valley.

Alan said that Justin was born with a natural high and that is why he neither drank nor did drugs. When I returned home from the U.S. after a divorce, Alan became my only friend too. Justin then stopped coming to Alan's room.

In later years, he told me that Alan's friendship was one more thing I robbed him of in his life.

ALAN'S ROOM

Alan's room was at the opposite end of the apartment from his mother's. It had two private entrance doors—one off the main stairway and one off his bathroom. Alan's friends or lovers came in through one door and left through another.

He painted at night under fluorescent light. The paintings showed muscular black men with fluorescent erections defying women with oversized feet. He played Barry White CDs, served Folgers coffee with cream, amphetamines, joints, and Baby Ruth chocolate bars.

When he feared I might despise him for his homosexuality, he taunted me: "I know how to please a man better than any woman," he said. "Honey, my ass is the best pussy any man will ever feel. Trust me. You think that having a vagina gives you the advantage? Bet you have no idea how to use it. I am so good I can blow smoke-rings out of my ass and suck them back in. And my mouth can make a man come until his brain blows all the fuses in the box and he begs for his mama. And even the mama will want some. To please a man, you have to want a man. You have to want him so much you sweat, I mean sweat, and you have to feel that your whole blood is running out. Me, I can look at a man's hand and I start to sweat. I am that good."

"Do you sweat for Justin?" I asked.

"I used to. But it's a waste—he is not gay. Now, I just love him."

ALAN'S FRIENDS

There was Patrick, whose high-society mulatto parents had finally disowned him because he married a woman whose only good use in his life, they thought, would be as a nanny. It was enough for them that they had endured the shame of having him locked up at Pont Bedèt Mental Asylum for two years. Patrick said that he spent his days shaking the asylum's gate with the other inmates, shouting insults at anyone in the streets. He claimed he had a hell of a grand time there until the doctor decided that he was not at all insane and was just living it up for free. His parents complained bitterly to all who would hear it that as soon as Patrick was discharged from the asylum he went and married a fat black woman twenty years older than him and with whom he quickly adopted a fat black baby girl, whom he had the audacity to show off around town to all who would see it and on days when he was not otherwise parading around the Port-au-Prince cemetery with the Freemasons in full black satin regalia under the midday sun.

Then, there was Hilda. Alan called her "Red"—she had the worst henna job you ever saw on a sixty-year-old woman with body fat overflowing out of clothes that could only have been made for a fifteen-year-old who loves bright colors. Red was French. Alan and Red communicated together in their own adaptation of Kreyòl. She worked as a whore in Paris until the day she married the black Haitian pimp she adored—he needed a French work permit and so he swore eternal love to her. She believed him.

After the wedding, Hilda got herself flown to Port-au-Prince and dumped in a rented bordello room alone with the five dogs for which she'd have given her life. The Haitian pimp went back to France with his new French passport.

The best Hilda could do after he left was to rent herself a shack high up in the mountains of Kenskoff—two bare rooms with floors always wet from the constant mopping of dog piss, and where she subsisted on day-old bread bought with money she earned by embroidering pink doilies that sold in high-class boutiques.

There was also Reynaldo, a dashing upper-class mulatto who lived off the family money made by his father as an army officer and, later in life, as a high-ranking diplomat in Paris. For years, Alan swapped lovers with Reynaldo during sex parties. He last saw him stretched on a thin bed at the Canape Vert Hospital, dying of AIDS.

There was fifteen-year-old Gerard who had a studied elegance as he smoked nonchalantly on the back stairway near Alan's room. He was a beautiful youth with perfect black skin whom Alan truly loved and who died of AIDS.

There was Jonas, black with hair, dreams, and anger, spitting insults and poetry, dripping red paint on canvases made out of wheat sacks, demanding that the cowardly world finally admit to his artistic genius. Still full of dreams and anger, he died of AIDS.

There was the cream-colored lover Alan never called by any other name than "my cream-colored," only to protect him because that one was married with children, living in a shack. Alan liked to think that Cream-Colored was doing it for love, not for money, and so that made it an act of destiny when he too died of AIDS.

There was Jacques, who chauffeured for Alan's mother and who was too beautiful for Alan to resist asking him to pose in the nude for his fluorescent paintings of black men, just so he could sweat and watch the fellow, suddenly dressed up in silks, fall in love with himself.

There was Justin, smooth as a peach when he was young and looking like innocence itself taking form in a man.

And there was me.

JUSTIN'S ROOMS

Alan's old room was eventually walled off from his mother's apartment after they had both gone back to Miami to die. First it was Alan who left to get AIDS treatment in a U.S. hospital and then it was Betty because her son had died and she wanted to go home.

Alan's old room became Justin's room. It still had two possible entrances or exits.

Justin had been living in the slums ever since our father had kicked him out of the valley. He had stayed in a shack with his wife until he was also booted out of there.

People in the slums resented, disrespected, and distrusted a man rejected by his own wealthy family, forced into life on an earthen floor, in a single-room hut with no running water, identical to their own. They didn't accept this unwanted witness to a dejected poverty they could not avoid and which shamed them, nor did they want the constant presence of one who was not of their world, would never be, and could escape at the first opportunity. They also had the instinct of wild animals that sniff out the odd one, the deformed or the weak, and leave him to die from heat, cold, or hunger.

Justin himself soon grew weary of these people who threw rocks at him when he stood in the morning lines at the water fountain to fill up his buckets. He argued bitterly with his wife who, in time, also began to throw rocks at him and finally left.

He was happy to be accepted back in the valley, back in a room full of memories of his friend, even if the walls were vastly water-stained and the bathroom in such disrepair that no one would have rented it while my father refused to spend any money to fix it.

Justin liked the two doors—one to the stairs to the lobby and the other out the bathroom to the garden. This way, he had a choice of exits depending on where he was running off to or whom he was trying to avoid.

He laid his emaciated body on the bed, alone all day in a room that used to be full of life. He projected his fantasies on the walls and these kept him from feeling the weight of the low ceiling overhead.

His wife eventually reappeared, several months pregnant.

Once our father had died, I too came back to the valley. I found that Justin was now out of Alan's room. He had moved into my father's studio apartment, and was sleeping in the big bed next to which he once slept for months, lying on a thin floor mattress to watch over his father, who suffered from anxiety attacks at night. He stayed in the apartment long enough, and had enough time on his hands, to secretly sell, one by one, every single thing that was in the apartment: rugs, furniture, paintings, clothes, television, knickknacks, fridge, and dishes, saving the bed for last. Finally, he pawned Father's gold ring at a Vodou priest's and moved back into the childhood room he profoundly detested.

He grew up in a blue room hoping all the while that it were painted pink, like mine.

Every night, Justin drags a thin foam mattress to the grassy plateau where he buried his son.

Each night, he picks a different tree under which to lie down, as one would pick a friend to visit.

WHITE PAINT

Nowadays, all of the valley rooms are painted white—it makes them easier to repair, scrub, scrape, and cover up with fresh paint while Drylok paint seals and hides old water stains.

Alan's and Justin's old room is now the office from which I manage the apartments for the family.

Calendars and accounting charts replace Alan's fluorescent paintings of male erections. The double-sided mahogany desk that was built for Justin and me in our adolescence is standing in the place of Alan's bed. It is the very desk where Justin used to sit face to face with me in our study room overlooking the pool and stare at my growing breasts instead of doing homework. At this desk I now face an accountant who constantly glances at me to check if I am watching over him.

A gray fan stirs the hot, humid air.

Outside the window, I catch a glimpse of Justin, who is looking into the room from under a palm tree while he eats cookies. Grief always hovers in the room but I am never sure whose it is.

POSTCARDS

A few days ago, Mr. Lemarguet was just out of the pool and sponging himself when I walked nearby and waved. He works at the French embassy and had just returned from visiting his family. He said he wasted his last three days home with worry and grief over the separation that was again to come.

That morning, I watched a few tourists in downtown Port-au-Prince while they were buying postcards at the main post office. One man must have bought a good thirty postcards and, standing in the crowded room, he proceeded to write on them. No matter how many he had already bought, he needed more. He went back to the stacks of postcards to select others and was never satisfied with having found the perfect one. It seemed that with each postcard sent, a little part of him would be gone.

Each postcard represented a person I did not know and would never meet. I thought that each postcard had the same shape and purpose of rooms meant to hold secrets.

Mr. Lemarguet hurriedly covered his legs with a towel when I walked by.

He stood at the spot where my father once stood on hairy legs that stuck out of a navy bathing suit my mother hated because it looked to her like a skirt. It is the spot where Betty had sighed over her legs that used to be pretty but were scarred from the car accident that nearly killed her; the spot where Alan laid his own legs under the midday sun to get a nice tan; the spot where Mrs. Prioré nowadays lies down to try out the effect of her new yellow bikini and gossips about other teachers at the French school with Mrs. Jean-Baptiste who checks on her cellulite.

It is the spot where Bluet Prioré jumps in the water with both little legs tight together so they make a loud splash because she intends to destabilize and snatch the inflatable dinosaur on which her sister Jade proudly parades.

By now, where I stand, I feel that life has taken the parading out of me. People's lives have left water marks on the walls and blind spots over the sun.

My heart lets out repeated laments like the chorus in an antique tragedy.

CHORUS LAMENT

I spread a clean sheet on a grassy spot in the garden. I lie on it as I did in childhood, talking to clouds and counting them. I had as many friends then as I could count clouds. Now, I close my eyes to count the days.

I tell myself stories about what will happen when these unfriendly days end and I can exit the past.

Dusk applies its damp fingers on the earth and black flies polkadot the low grass.

The incessant howl of a cat in heat sounds like a baby's cries.

The sky paints a yellow screen above our heads. The ocean sparkles with thousands of golden eyes.

SUNDAY LUNCH

I hear my mother cough. It is such an old, single, lonesome cough in the distance.

Time has dissolved the features of the mother I knew. Yet a singular perfection is replacing her former beauty. It is as if her features go to feed a growing spiritual image that hovers over her progressively withering body.

However, she is not interested in the new imprint of her soul over her face—her face's skin is a fabric she mends daily with makeup she applies with painstaking accuracy.

In the mirror, she observes the black hole her life makes caving in on itself. She can't hold it up the efficient way her dentures hold her mouth up. But, no matter; after she dies, memory will send us perfect postcards of her.

Mother likes food she can mold. She always serves us, her children, deviled eggs on Sundays. They taste like lavender.

She is so concerned about the smells of old age that she lavishes eau de cologne on herself constantly during the day. She pours an amount in her cupped hands and then splashes it on noisily, breathing it in deeply. So whatever food her hands prepare, it tastes like perfume—even garlic bread, her favorite. Wherever her hands touch me, her fingerprints remain as eau de cologne. She asks me how I like her food. I don't tell her the truth anymore. It matters more to me that she feels happy and proud. She needs to feed her sense of worth by being acknowledged as a good cook and an effective mother. If I mention the lavender flavor she'd say that, as usual, I enjoy criticizing and belittling her. Justin would be quick to agree.

He somehow does not notice the perfumed flavor of the dishes she prepares. He is always famished and eats anything she puts on his plate, large amounts, slowly, interminably.

If our mother serves me one more deviled egg than she does him, one more mouthful of any dish, if she asks my opinion about her cooking before she asks for his, he becomes livid, his lips tighten and words come out of his mouth like a growl.

In judging me difficult to please, Mother finds my compliments harder to obtain and thus somehow more satisfying than Justin's. She therefore never gives up trying to make me eat extra morsels. In this way, she puts me in conflict with Justin; he understands I am, in an odd way, being favored over him.

Justin's competitive, watchful eyes tie knots in my stomach and kill my appetite more thoroughly than the lavender does. Sitting at the table, I try hard to manage what seem to our mother only a few reluctant mouthfuls. Whatever I agree to swallow, it is always an amount insufficient to what she would perceive as a good enough compliment.

After we get up from the table, I stay a while and try to make small talk that might repair her renewed disappointment of the lunch she served us. I tell her she looks particularly pretty and youthful that day. She smiles gratefully.

In a corner of the room, the stray dog that recently adopted my mother and, going one day at a time, managed to remain, is watching me. I don't pat him anymore because he takes any gesture as an invitation to jump my leg, pink penis erect. When I push him away in disgust, Mother tells me that I am a prude.

She often likes to add that I am wasting the brief privileges of youth by covering up my breast and dressing up in long skirts and sleeves like an old maid. She means to give me good advice. She warns me that men like women who dress sexy. When she criticizes me, Justin chuckles in his seat.

When I leave, she walks me out. She tells me that I must try and understand Justin. Mother ends her Sunday feeling she has again failed, and I do too.

MEALS

It is over meals at the table that, as a child, I would get a chance to observe my parents together. We ate in silence in front of an abundance of food laid before us. The silence was not one—there were three distinct silences.

There was my father's silence, distinct from ours because of the disquiet it brought us. It was made even more ominous by the burdens of the day, albeit unspoken, which we felt were weighing inside him, and to which we believed we contributed heavily.

There was the silence in which my mother and brother were joined as accomplices in fear of saying anything that would irritate Father and bring him to make renewed disparaging comments about them, their lack of intelligence or overall incompetence in anything being the chosen ones. Father blamed Mother for the dissatisfying lack of character he found in Justin and reminded her that he was *her* son. Mother's silence was an anxious watch over Justin's and her survival.

The third silence was my own. And it persists, even in their absence.

SISTERS

"Hellò! Good afternoon Madame! See what I got for Christmas?" says six-year-old Bluet with a smile.

She has the golden eyes of a sunny day while she shows me

a naked Barbie doll in between whose plastic breasts she holds a proud proprietary small index finger. Before I am able to congratulate Bluet, I hear an angry voice.

"Bluet! Where is my mask?" cries Jade from the pool terrace, interrupting Bluet's pleasure in showing off her new doll.

"I already told you it is at the bottom of the pool and that I am going to get it back for you!" Bluet answers.

"You better get it right now! It's not *your* mask, it's mine!" Jade says.

"Well!" says Bluet. "If that's the way you're going to be, I am going to go to my room right now and I am going to lock the door!"

"Bluet!"

AT THE POOL

Head bent forward, right arm hanging by his side, left arm raised straight up with the palm of the hand opened towards the sky, Justin stands on legs exactly one foot apart. He is perfectly still, stiller still than the surface of the pool in this breathless morning.

Bluet and Jade are walking to the pool in their bathing suits and holding loaded water pistols pointed forward.

Jade's pistol is purple and orange. Bluet's is pink and green. The girls are ten and six.

Jade has tucked her swimming flippers under her free arm while Bluet flaps around wearing hers and follows her sister, shooting water at her from behind. She holds an inflatable dinosaur at the throat, tucked under her armpit. The rest of its multigreen body drags over the ground and its bottom bounces with each quick step Bluet takes.

Bluet suddenly notices Justin and stops.

She runs quickly ahead of Jade, dinosaur bobbing furiously, to get a closer look at him. Then, she turns around with her index finger stiff and pressed to her puckered lips, and motions Jade to be quiet. Finally, with a determined step, she gets very close to Justin.

Standing as she is, in front of him who is tall, she fits perfectly just beneath him whose head is bent down, thus allowing her to stare him straight in the eyes.

She stays quiet for a while and then can no longer resist: "What are you doing?" she asks.

"Chinese meditation," he says, slowly.

"What's that?"

"Focusing on the balance between yin and yang."

Bluet pauses silently for a brief moment. She then runs back to Jade and whispers in her ear. They both fall silent and turn to stare at Justin.

Justin then stretches both arms in front of him and begins to move all his fingers, checking their motion one at a time. He then makes tight fists that he opens and shuts, slowly, repeatedly. He raises his head and looks in the direction where Bluet and Jade are still watching him. Finally, he moves his legs and starts walking toward them.

When he gets close, he pulls out a piece of coconut from his pants pocket and hands it to Bluet. Jade bites her nails.

"Coconut is yin," Justin says. "Water is yin, the moon is yin, women are yin. The sun is yang. Men are yang—Chinese people have divided everything between yin and yang."

While Justin is speaking, Bluet has spotted her father coming to the pool. Before Justin can continue his commentary further, Bluet runs to him with great excitement.

"Papa, Papa! Justin has given me a piece of yin! Here, taste it first!"

CHORUS LAMENT

Love is a violin whose strings resound deep in the place where fetuses lie.

The day retreats to savor what has passed and prepares for a night that advances with iguana steps.

Love holds a matador's red flag in my dreams.

Hill dogs howl.

When we were girls, Mathilde told me that when we get old we get the face we deserve.

Now that we sit once more together in the valley, her left eye is a fake and her once sinuous lips have a singular upward distortion. The adolescent boy shot her because she saw him first, stealing into the house he thought empty. She saw when he pointed the gun at her—she started lifting her Bible from the desktop in front of which she was standing. The bullet aimed at her heart was sent off course by the hardbound book. It went through her eye instead, and up her forehead.

Mathilde was born with a face like a perfect prayer.

At the hospital, I sat by her bedside. She held my hand and, ushering sounds with difficulty through swollen lips and jaws, she told me, "You look . . . so very pretty . . . today . . ."

After she left the hospital, she took to wearing dark sunglasses outside. At the house, she stuck black tape over the left side of her reading glasses. With these daily new measures quietly established, she waited for the fake eye that was being prepared for her.

The day came when she flew to the U.S. for the final fitting of the new eye. The Chinese eye painter had to sit astride her body laid stiffly on a bed while he was painting her new glass eye already put in place in the healed eye socket. He held a miniature paintbrush with his right hand, and a magnifying glass over her good eye with his left hand, so he could copy it and paint an identical match on the glass ball that was to become Mathilde's left eye until the day she died.

With her one and real eye, Mathilde quietly stared at the eyes with the mysterious, narrow slant that were examining her so delicately and would imprint her so deeply. She prayed.

Nowadays however, when her right eye looks at you, the glass eye looks elsewhere. When her right eye blinks, the left stares ahead.

The glass eye that sits in the empty socket seems an inner eye focused on the soul of things. The emptied eye socket filled with an eye that looks where no one else does is a kind of inner space Life had reserved for her to probe, a space uniquely and intimately hers. It is the room, the stage, where her soul met with her strength. It is the room where she shows a heart alien to bitterness, the room where her power rests after she has surrendered everything.

She now lives as one who has died but returned. At night, she curls into this empty space and thanks God for having had this chance to understand His sacrifice. Her laughter is now loudest in any room in which she stands. When she answers the phone, she says, "Hello! I am here."

It is my turn to wonder: which face did my mother grow to deserve?

When I look at her face I realize that I have long lost her. Her faces through the ages of our lives had so many covers of red and rouge and white and mascara that I find I never knew the one underneath.

When I catch her unprepared and showing the face usually hidden beneath the colors, I see that it too has become a mask.

Where has she gone? When did I lose my mother? Was she ever mine or is it only me that is hers? The first syllable of the name she gave me is the feminine French proprietary one—"ma."

However, the confusion about faces is only mine. My mother has no doubt about the face of life she wants.

"I want to live," she says, "even if I must crawl around on all four. I want to live at all cost!"

Morning time, when she puts on the red and the rouge and the white and the mascara, is the time when birds sing loudest outside her bedroom windows on the side of which her father's death mask is hung. His eyes are forever shut in the white plaster while she underlines hers with black lines so they look bigger, brighter, revealing appetite.

Mathilde knows how a death mask is made.

"One must be extremely careful while removing the plaster off the corpse's face," she says. "Any slight pull of the plaster on one side more than the other and the lips will have a twist."

When Justin sings, his eyes, raised to the sky, take on the glow of moons. His hands are cupped like a bouquet under his throat.

He feels the surge of sounds up his body as if it were a child needing to emerge, be delivered, and born into musical hands.

IN THE NAME OF THE FATHER

It was a funny-looking Christ figure I once planted into the ground at our front door where it remained until water and worms rotted the wood and toppled it over.

With a bare potbelly, a shroud across the hips, arms joined together upward and nailed to the cross, the Christ sculpture oddly looked like a carnival frolicker lifting his ecstatic arms to exhibit flesh.

During his afternoon rounds, Mrs. Prioré's dog commonly walks by the spot where the Christ used to be, and stops to piss there. This dog sometimes disappears for days at a time. He yet reappears miraculously looking well and not hungry.

After he has pissed at the spot of the cross, the dog scouts around with an agenda only known to him. He first follows the tracks my mother's car tires make on the grassy plateau where Justin sleeps every night and where his son is buried.

She insists on crossing through the plateau with the car even though a good driveway is to the side and the tracks, like long and irreversible scars, spoil the plateau's virgin grass and prettiness.

The dog then enters the dense bed of tall *zorèy bourik* plants and lies low, out of sight, until I get bored watching him and no longer care what he does next.

TO THE SON A FATHER

The baby's mother, Justin's wife, had been a wiry, pretty girl. She also was a brazen, defiant little shrew, albeit one with a big heart.

She sent everything she earned to the mother who never raised her.

Very early in her childhood, she had been given away to be

a servant to an old, unfeeling, miser aunt, veritable fairy-tale witch-creature who gave the small girl very little food and never a chance to go to school.

My father had thrown Justin out of the house because of her. He had never met the girl until she once unexpectedly came to the valley, caught sight of him walking coincidentally in her direction, picked up a rock, threw it at his face, hit him in the forehead with it, laughed and left.

My father felt the blood running down and started to shout.

Justin came back to the valley without his wife. They had tried a life together in the slums, against all odds. The odds won.

When she turned up again several months later, he went to plead with his father for her to be allowed to stay in the room with him. She was such a skinny girl that it was only in the last month that her pregnancy became visible. Had it been noticeable earlier, it would not have made a difference because Father both refused to see her or let her stay.

"Over my dead body!" Justin's father said to his son's plea.

A body did turn up—Justin buried his son, flesh of his father's flesh, the only grandchild my father ever had.

In later years, my father's green eyes turned gray. He was a long time silent when he learnt about his grandson.

"I never knew," he said. "I am sorry." He bent his head and looked down at his hands.

It was not clear if he cried. The only times I saw my father cry are those when he would speak of his mother, long after she had died.

MOTHER TO A CHILD

After the child died, the child's mother left Justin once again and it seemed we would never see her again. She went back to working on the streets.

But when Father died, the girl reappeared in the valley, announcing she was going to the funeral.

She said she was family. She reminded us that our father was her father-in-law and that, considering his new "station" in life, there wasn't much he could do against her anymore. Father, however, long before he died in the accident, had already taken all steps with his lawyers to ensure that she would not ever be able to claim him as father-in-law. Justin was legally divorced and didn't know it.

The girl said that she did not care and money was not what she was after.

"Why does she come then?" the family asked with worry. "What is she going to do? Isn't she into Vodou? She'll put a spell somewhere! She wants to shame us! Curse us! A street girl! A peasant! We can't let her come! She has the foulest mouth! But how do we stop her? A church is a public place. Dear God! Justin only brings trouble."

The girl must have spent at least a whole month's earnings from prostituting herself on the streets to be able to buy the long, black, shimmering evening gown in which she entered the church the day of my father's funeral.

She walked alone, holding her chin up, down the aisle along which all heads turned, wealthy mulatto faces, until she stood in front of Father in his coffin, slowly cross-signed herself, and bowed her head. Then she joined the line of people who proceeded to pay their respects to the family.

Uncles and aunts, cousins, close friends of the family, some of them Ministers of State, we all shook hands with her.

Justin was the one who had gone to tell her that Father had died. He was lonely and missed her. He spent much of his time looking for her, asking about her and following her trail on the Port-au-Prince streets.

"What's your problem you're looking for me like this? Am I your mother or something?" she'd yell at him. "What did you bring me? What have you got for me? What! Cookies and small change? Again!"

When things got worse and she fell deathly ill, Justin was right there by her side and she accepted his help. He packed her few things. He accompanied her on the long, hot, bumpy bus ride that took her to her hometown in the south where she wanted to die.

"She had personality and she was a saint," Justin said to me.

"She took destitute girls in with us. Yet, we had nothing. She still kept doing it when we were not living together anymore. She gave them food, a place to sleep, her own clothes even. But she always ended up having to kick them out—street kids are ruthless—they use you, they don't thank you, they end up robbing you. It's real life out there. All I have is peanuts. The day God made my wife is the day he was making real people. She did not die of a natural death—people did magic against her—she was the best at her work and the most beautiful; they did not want her to get ahead; people never do. But one thing I know for sure, she did not shed a tear for herself before she died."

TALKING BULL

In the town of Jacmel, there was a bull that spoke. He said that he had three children and needed to find his way back home. One day, a man called Kasanyòl whispered in the bull's ears and the bull dropped dead.

And now, there is a popular saying used as a threat: "Watch out or I'll say to you what Kasanyòl said to the bull."

In the valley, a tall breadfruit tree fell. It wasn't the long rain that uprooted it but the wind after the rain.

What did wind whisper to the tree?

The gray, scarred tree trunk stretches and lies across three succeeding garden terraces, like a bridge over generations.

The breadfruit tree isn't useful wood so it's hard to find someone that will agree to come chop and take it away.

Joceline, the washerwoman, puckers her lips and looks away each time she passes by the tree while taking her load of clean clothes up the stairways to the main house.

A tree laid down is like a bull that talks—it is against nature.

She carries the basket full of freshly ironed clothes high on her head, like folded flags in witness to her power against stains, marks, and scars, as if cloth is skin she can wash and repair. When Kasanyòl whispers, Joceline irons harder.

ICE CREAM

Justin comes down the alley to the gate with an ice cream bar. He licks his fingers to clean up what's melting down. It's green ice cream.

He says to me, "I bumped into cousin Willy and I told him I go to the Protestant church now. But he already knew. He said you told him. You talk too much."

Two chickens, as if following the same beat, walk on the bald pathway that separates the lawn like two sides of a brain. I am watching them from the terrace where I stand with my mother who is eating ice cream. A lizard nearing her foot suddenly stops. It nods its head as it swells the thin underside of its green chin. A breeze agitates the tree foliage overhead.

My mother spoon-sucks her pistachio ice cream topped with a high-rise of cream and a cherry. She licks the corners of her old mouth where ice cream oozes down caked lipstick.

She tells me, "Whatever happens in life, never regret anything."

CHORUS LAMENT

Shantideva said:

> "Although I may live happily for a long time
> Though obtaining a great deal of material wealth,
> I shall go forth empty-handed and destitute
> Just like having been robbed by a thief."

THE GROTTO

Death does not create an absence. Once it has visited you, it never leaves. It remains and dies anew each day.

Each ensuing day adds to death, enhances its shape, bulk, and weight.

You think you are alone in a room but Death is here. It acts like water that slowly rises in the room, nearing the ceiling. There is little space left, and you try to stay above water. The ceiling is always too low, too close.

At times, instead of the water rising, it seems that it's the ceiling that is coming down and compressing.

The bed feels like a grave and you bolt out of it, fortunately still able to run, unlike those who are really dead and cannot get out, all those you love and miss, those who are packed under the earth, and you wonder all the time if the chickens all over the garden know what they are doing when they scratch the earth constantly and tear at it, as if moved by a spasm they can't control.

The worms caught in the chicken's beak wriggle hard because dark earth is where they belong. Tropical sunshine, for these creatures, means being held fast in a tight beak, even though they may very briefly understand, and temporarily be lured by, the warmth of color and the comfort felt from it.

The body of death swells with each life taken.

It eats up the room space in your brain even after it has already taken over every room in the house, so much so you can never be alone anywhere because everywhere death sits there with a belly full of your friends. But its body is felt in ways unlike the volume of normal things.

It is a grotto where the hollow itself is the body.

ODETTE

Odette now sits alone in her apartment, frail like an afterthought.

Her husband lived to be a withered shroud emptied of its mind, a man who could not remember he ever had a body.

Odette cleansed and caressed him until what remained in her arms was itself foreign to her, nothing she had known, not even his skin.

When he died, his forgotten body became present again and heavy as stone.

Little Catholic girls learn about relics—bits and pieces of beings that recall the whole.

When Odette sees what is left in her hands, she lets out a wail, so close to a bleat.

MOTHER'S WALK

Mother goes out for a walk—she locks her bedroom door, then the door to the terrace; she hobbles down to the second floor, clutching the railing.

When she was young, she had long slender fingers with red fingernails. She still likes to coquettishly rest a hand on her hip when she poses for a photograph, like she did for me when I was a little girl dazzled dumb by her beauty, and wanting to take her image with the children's camera I received for Christmas.

The very first photo I took of life was of my mother.

She stood like a vamp in front of our green house with red lipstick on, hand resting on hip. But the film was black and white. Her lips and flowered skirt came out in disappointing shades of gray.

Once she is outside, passing by the car garage, Mother avoids dog shit that's dried up and shriveled black like Chinese calligraphy on gray cement.

Once in the garden, she walks past my father's grave without looking, even though I planted flowers there. She reaches the gate and unties the faded scarf that keeps the two sides shut and goes on to tread with a hesitant foot over the rest of the property.

She follows the tracks that her car's tires have made on the grassy plateau. Her skirt flowers over the green around her and frightens the chickens. They scatter. She eventually gets near the uprooted breadfruit tree that fell a few days ago. Its roots, tendrils, tentacles, intestines, and wormy guts are all displayed and seem to grab at her eyes. She stops.

She pauses and looks a long, silent moment because it has been a long, arduous descent before she finds herself standing at this fallen tree.

Jade and Bluet are taking a walk on an upper terrace, pushing a baby carriage. They've dressed the doll laid to sleep in the carriage with soft woolens as if for winter and its rubber face smiles pink under a cap. The pull-shade is down so the baby won't suffer from the sun.

"Oh the sun! How I love the sun!" my mother told me once. "It warms me. It bites me. It fills my whole body. I have become a nudist for it! I offer myself to it, in the morning, in the afternoon, all day. I literally lick the sun up in my skin. When I go out, I can't wait to come back home. I take everything off my body, every bit of clothing, off! And I go again to feel the sun out on the terrace. It is changing my skin. It is changing me."

Bluet and Jade take sudden notice of my mother below.

They stop on their track and abruptly turn around. Then they continue on their walk, going the other way, and remain attentive to the baby doll, often rearranging its woolens to make sure it is comfortable and safe.

Bluet picks flowers on her way and arranges them like a necklace on the doll's chest.

"Hello little mothers!" I say. "Nice baby! Is it a boy or a girl?"

"A girl."

"What's her name?"

"Flora."

"Which one of you is her mother? Whose baby is she?"

"She belongs to a friend of ours. She is letting us have her for a week."

"Did she take anything in exchange?"

"No. Every time she comes over she never finds anything she likes, and all the music we have she already has."

"Where is Bluet's Barbie doll? Won't you take her out too?"

"This is a baby carriage. Barbie is a grown-up."

JUSTIN'S FAITH

Jesus has become Justin's passion.

Every Saturday and Sunday, he wakes up before dawn and dresses to go and climb for an hour the hills stretching behind the river slums, all the way up to a room with a tin roof where a young pastor holds services and offers prayers said to heal the sick.

The room is not large enough to hold all those who come and people stand outside. Everyone sings, claps, and prays as loudly as they can. Justin is the only white person there.

Men must wear long sleeves and a tie. The sun is as hot under the tin roof as it is outside over bare heads of people who pray with eyes closed while sweat runs down their faces.

The pastor mesmerizes with the passion of his sermons during which he elaborates on the significant mission for which he claims every human being comes on earth.

He has taken Justin under his wing. He has determined that my brother's talent is to lay hands on the sick and heal. He has convinced him that he must convert, turn his back on the Virgin Mary and the cohort of Catholic Saints and forever adhere to his Church. He has declared that Justin is to remain a loyal attendant to services performed there, and there only, if he is to find his true place in this world, be saved in the next.

Justin is preparing for his new baptism day with great excitement. He says that there will be nine new converts to be baptized together. He is the only Catholic of the group. The others come from the country provinces where Vodou traditions are strong.

On their baptism day, they will be dressed in all new white clothes and go make their vows at a place by the sea in which they will be immersed.

Justin now looks at my wooden Madonna statue and at my votive candles to different Saints as heretical, misguided worship. He spends his week writing songs for Jesus.

I hear him practicing them as he walks through the garden. Some days, he overcomes his discomfort with my Madonna and pays me a visit to ask my opinion about his newest song. He sits in the apartment with his back turned to the row of burning candles. His face lights up when I praise him. He confides in me about the sick he has visited and healed by laying his hands on them while singing his own songs in between reciting psalms.

Once, I went to the pastor's to join Justin there. He was happy to see me. He introduced me to the pastor and to the important male figures of that Church. The pastor held Justin by the shoulders as if to present him as his esteemed son when, instead, he was young enough to be Justin's son. The pastor treated me with interest until he realized I would not be coming back. I left the church feeling confident that Justin would eventually and sadly understand the real nature of the pastor's friendship.

The children were excited to meet Justin's sister and followed me a while to touch my hair, my hands, my purse.

There is an old woman who dresses only in red and blue as if she were the Haitian flag and who infrequently comes to see Justin. Her head tied in a scarf and her full knee-length skirt fanning around her skinny legs, she places her hands on Justin's head and prays over him while he kneels in front of her. I think she comes to do some of the pastor's work but I am not sure. I wait and see.

_____

TEARS

Jade and Bluet argue on the back stairs where Justin used to sit and watch into Alan's room when I was in there, and where Alan's friend Gerard used to practice smoking with elegance.

Jade wants to listen to CDs, play dress-up and dance merengue while Bluet wants to go read by herself in her room a new story-book she received from her mother. Jade sobs loudly. She is sitting on the steps while Bluet is standing next to her. She holds and pulls on Bluet's arm, begging her not to leave her, tears running into her distorted mouth.

Bluet hesitates, looking puzzled, and then sits next to Jade. She stares at her, speechless.

But in a short while, she springs back up and leaves abruptly. She walks toward their house without looking back. The bottom part of her bathing suit is pulled up to one side and one loose, rounded, small, springy buttock bounces over each impatient little step away she takes.

The mountaintop is capped with gray clouds. Leaves fallen off mahogany trees carpet the garden stairs and make over them a kind of damp, golden-brown collage of slivered eyes.

I take one leaf and press it on my forehead like a third eye. This morning drizzle feels like a benediction that pearls my hair. There is not a bird to be seen, not a sound to be heard, and trees sway in silence.

Earlier today, I lit a new votive candle for Saint Anthony, restorer of things lost, and my mother's favorite Saint.

She is forever losing her keys, forever promising to light him a candle if she finds them, forever forgetting her promises afterwards, and I wonder if her door to paradise hangs on that riddle.

The keys that I have lost are those to my life, home, and love.

I have lost eyes that light up when they see me and a skin fragrance that lingered in the palm of my hand.

I have lost the confident garden of childhood where I would lean on trees to focus on roots.

I have lost the mother who danced cha-cha-cha, the one who refused to kiss her small daughter because she was afraid to get attached to her or ruin her makeup. Lost the mother who thought that breasts have to be shown off, legs shown off, bare back shown off, nails lacquered red, and fingers covered with rings.

I lost the mother that seemed beyond my grasp, beyond beautiful, beyond love, beyond the mountain, beyond God even.

I have lost the youthful mother whose fears had not yet learnt to lasso around my own throat and pull. I have lost the father I should have had.

I have also lost the brother who sang at my wedding, sang because he was a bird, and because birds taught him. I lost the brother who had not yet developed a need to sing for Jesus, write for Jesus, and get on his knees every day, every night under the moon. I have lost moments, images, windows.

I have lost all rooms that had breath once.

I am full with empty.

I need to enter the room where all things lost are stored with grace. I will wear on my forehead a third eye that is not just a leaf collage.

CHORUS LAMENT

A quiet bird breathed in my heart as I walked down the alley to the house after a heavy rain.
Yet palm trees seemed wet with moonlight and not rain.
I wanted to curl down in the bushes, down beneath red crotons and *malanga* leaves drenched in darkness.
I wanted to lie on the softened earth, not be afraid at all . . . Not afraid . . . Never more.

BARBIE'S ROOM

Bluet and Jade have built a small hut. They used some smaller branches broken off the fallen tree. Inside the hut, they've laid Bluet's Barbie down on a flowered cloth.
I asked if Barbie could get wet and lonely.
"No," Bluet said, "she won't. She has a roof over her head and we've given her some toys. She'll be fine."
Yet, a black chicken right out of Jean's drawings and four times the size of Barbie entered the hut. At first, it seemed not to notice the doll but, suddenly, after a sideways glance, pecked at it.
Bluet chased after the chicken like an avenging God. She then told her mother that she needed to have her own dog to guard over her Barbie.
When I was her age, I had my own dog—Trotinette appeared at our doorstep, an abandoned dog. She was a black mixed-breed with the appearance of a dachshund. We adopted her and she adopted me. Long, low to the ground, her loose nipples flopping right and left, Trotinette followed me everywhere I walked.
One day, her belly started to swell and each additional day that

passed she looked more pregnant. Her breasts grew tight with milk. They no longer flopped but hung heavily and gray. Her eyes took on a humbled look.

Then, when Justin and I became more excited thinking that the time for her delivering puppies was getting really close, Trotinette's belly started progressively to lose its swelling. No puppies. The vet diagnosed her with having had a neurotic pregnancy.

TERAMÈN

I had not seen Teramèn for a couple of years when she suddenly showed up at the valley, looking as big as a house and dressed in a pink suit.

"I missed you; I had to see you," she said.

"I missed you too but I can't trust you anymore. You know why," I said.

Tears ran down her cheeks. Nothing else moved in her face. Tears streamed from silent, black pools sunk in whites that slowly turned to red.

"Do you know that Majeni had a baby?" she said, after a moment. "She is not with the man any more, but his family helps with the baby. She is eighteen now. She quit school. Rozmèn did too. I guess the money you were giving us for tuitions and books was really spent somewhere else."

"Teramèn," I said, "all along, you schemed with your children."

"You were right to be angry," she said.

"I was sad, not angry," I said. "You were dishonest."

"Yes . . ." she said quietly, then added, "But, about Majeni, the man came to see me to ask about going out with her. I told him she was not old enough to start with love. He forced himself on her. The baby girl is now three years old. Her name is Meji."

"Couldn't Majeni have fought the man?" I asked. "Couldn't she have screamed? There are people everywhere in the slums where you live. It's hard to be alone, hard to be raped with no one at least hearing what is going on, especially if there is a struggle. She must have been willing."

"Must have," Teramèn said. "Love is all she thinks about. If I say anything against what they want to do, my girls accuse me of being mean and wanting to control them. I can't make them understand that there is nothing good for them in love. And now, Rozmèn is pregnant too. She is not yet fifteen. Love, that's all they see. They are excited about it. And I don't know how to tell them there is nothing there really."

"Did you ever finish building your house?" I asked.

"No," she said. "Just that one room still is where we live."

A MODEL TO DRAW

When Jean was a young man, he was the neighborhood slums' best domino player. Teramèn was one of the girls who habitually watched the men play. He knew that I wanted a model for drawing and he brought her over.

She needed money—she was pregnant with her first child and the man had already run off.

She had a discreet presence and was uncomplicated about being nude. I gave her milk and peanut butter sandwiches at the start of every drawing session. The only way to keep her awake was to keep her standing.

But even when she was no longer pregnant she'd fall asleep during reclining poses. I never knew if it was from being generally underfed or from being busy digesting the thick sandwiches I fed her.

Alan thought her the oddest creature. The drawing sessions were organized in his room. He'd dress Teramèn up with his Japanese kimono or with his mother's lounging robes. He constructed elaborate headdresses with brocade scarves over and around her head. He gave her carved staffs to lean on, African masks to hold in front of her face, and sharp machetes to brandish. He showed her how to lie with one breast and one leg sticking out of the dress, stretched like an odalisque over his animal skin bedspread, while we listened to Barry White sing on a cassette, "Honey, let's get it on."

She easily took all the poses found in European art as if they were out of the common aesthetic and sensibility of a girl from the Haitian slums. Yet, with her black skin emerging out of gold and white fabrics, and one hand holding staff, scepter, machete, or mask, she seemed truer to herself than the girl who at the end would slip back into her own faded dress.

When Alan and I organized an evening garden party for friends, Teramèn came and sat with us all afternoon, watching the goat that was being roasted whole over a fire in a pit dug deep in the earth. Guests were asked to dress in long exotic robes.

Alan came wearing his kimono. Teramèn recognized it only as the dress she had worn while posing for us and giggled irresistibly while she watched him walking regally down the stairs to the lower part of the garden where the pit had been dug.

He refused to eat any of the meat because, while taking a walk in the garden the day before, he had caught sight of the goat tied to a tree over one of the terraces.

"I cannot eat an animal I met and into whose eyes I have looked," he declared emphatically.

Justin agreed with him and also kept his plate away from the pit over which the cooked goat was being carved into slices and served. Teramèn, however, ate more meat in that one night than she might have in a month.

Blind and delirious from advanced AIDS and talking with me over the phone from his bed at the Miami hospice shortly before he died, Alan thought that he still was in his river valley room. That room in which he had been so alive was, in his mind, the same one in which he was dying.

"At what time is Teramèn coming?" he said. "Shouldn't we get ready?"

CHORUS LAMENT

I know the moon is not advancing in the sky but it seems so. It is the clouds that do move, solemn and slow, a procession of old men who draw the calm night shut in the background like curtains of a stage after the play has ended.

Bold moon presents a bare, full, undressed face.
Tonight's moon wants a clean slate sky.

GALLIC WINGS

There is a little boy who now comes often to play with Jade and
Bluet. When he arrives, even coconut trees seem to be dressed in
celebration, with their high-up clusters of orange fruits like bal-
loons hung for a party.

Bluet puts on a Gallic helmet with yellow wings. Each of her
hands is fitted with a brightly colored Sesame Street monster
puppet.

Jade fetches her red sword. A tight body shirt clings to her bud-
ding breasts.

Jade and Bluet both run after the boy and hurl threats at him.
The boy screams but lets them catch up with him.

From the pool, Justin calls out to them and dares the girls to try
and catch up with him instead.

DEPOT ROOM

Seven rooms had been built by my father with the intention of
renting them by the day, like a hotel does.

Alan's room had been such a room until my father decided to
connect it to the one-bedroom apartment adjacent to it. It had
been room number two.

Room number seven is now a depot filled with furniture carefully stacked almost to the ceiling. It is a room filled with things
that recount other rooms.

The washerwoman, Joceline, uses it for ironing. A small space
near an electric plug was cleared of furniture so she can do her
work alone and without distraction from other people.

Joceline does her work to perfection. She is a highly religious
woman with elevated moral standards but she is totally antisocial.

She does not like chatting with other workers. They feel her disdain and thus dislike her as well.

Ever since the neighborhood began having consistent electrical blackouts during the day, Joceline started sleeping in the depot on a floor mat she brought over. The electricity comes on at night on an irregular schedule, with unpredictable frequency or length of time. When the electricity comes on, the room's single bare lightbulb above the ironing board glares in Joceline's face and wakes her up. She gets up and irons until the electricity is again interrupted.

Joceline lives with her two daughters in the slums by the river. I asked her what she would like from the depot, which is crowded with furniture that no one in the family wants but all somehow cannot part with.

"The stove!" she said.

She wanted the stove. I agreed and she said she would have it picked up on the next Sunday.

Joceline showed up dressed for church and smelling of fresh cologne. She wore a black skirt and a high-collared white lace blouse, a black hat, purse, and high-heel shoes.

The hired pickup truck I expected turned out to be a man. He lifted the stove and carried it away on his back while Joceline giggled joyfully at seeing my stunned expression and gaping mouth.

I sat on the floor of the depot after Joceline had left with the stove. I looked at the things around me in a room I felt to be shrill, but that she likes for its quiet. Joceline can enjoy solitude in this room filled with furniture because none of it speaks to her.

Yet there was my father's huge carved mahogany desk, at which he sat for forty of his adult working years in his air-conditioned downtown Port-au-Prince office. Above the desk had hung a photo of his father wearing a bow tie. Under the glass top protection of the desk, my father had inserted a calendar photograph of vast tulip fields in Holland.

In the depot in which I lingered, feeling raw, I also noticed my parents' dining table set. I sat on one of these four chairs three times a day during all of my growing years. No one was ever invited for dinner, so there was never a need for more than four chairs.

I felt with my hand the things in the depot that were near me and then got up to leave. I caressed the entrance door, strong, and made of carved mahogany like all the other doors in the valley.

I remembered Anòl, the craftsman who set up his workshop at the bottom end of the garden to do all the woodwork now found in the valley rooms—doors, windows, beds, mirrors and picture frames, wall paneling, Justin's and my double-sided desk, and even a rocking chair built specially for my father, who suffered from back pains, and designed to copy John F. Kennedy's rocker in the White House.

Father sat in it in early evenings and read the *New York Times*. Feeling the door made me remember the man who made it, but also all the people who opened it to enter and inhabit room number seven.

Through the furniture kept in it, it can be said that this room is a room filled with other rooms.

But it is also a room filled with its own memory.

Father had not kicked Justin out of the valley just once but several times. During those times when he was not welcome, there were nights when Justin would nevertheless sneak back and ask Monklè, the man entrusted with all the valley room keys, to open room number seven for him.

I bumped into him there one night during one of my visits home from abroad. The night was hot and Justin had left the door open for more air. He was asleep and I watched him for a brief, silent moment. He slept with a black cloth covering his eyes and part of his face.

Justin felt my presence and woke up, startled. We sat on the doorstep together, chatting in conspiratorial tones and enjoying sharing the secret of his presence in the valley room.

He told me that the black cloth was both for darkness and for privacy from invisible eyes. I told him that every night I laid a black cloth on my eyes for the same reasons. He laughed with me.

Room number seven is also where I suffered my first bout of anxiety attacks.

My mother had been using my bedroom in the house since I had gone away to the U.S. and once, when I came home, she prepared room number seven for me instead of giving me my room back. She had enjoyed having her own room, albeit only as a daytime boudoir.

The walls in room seven had a pink flower wallpaper then. She had put carnations in a vase next to the bed but the ceiling was low and seemed lower each night I slept there until I could no longer. My father took me to his psychiatrist and was disappointed when I refused medication. Soon afterward, Justin started using this room whenever he could, while I never did again.

Monklè has been with the family since we were children. He has many children toward whom he was a responsible father, but we never saw them around while we grew up.

Lola is a daughter he had outside marriage with a previous washerwoman who worked in the valley before Joceline. She has her mother's green eyes, luminous and surprising in a dark complexion. After her mother lost her job in the valley, Lola remained there with her father. They lived in room number seven for a while. I don't remember when or why. But Lola kept chickens in the valley. She would call and throw corn kernels for them while she stood in the doorway. She talked to the chickens the same way I did when I too was a child.

In those days, there were servant quarters behind room number seven. One of the servant rooms was used as a coal kitchen and that is where the cook killed the chicken she served us later in Creole sauce at the mahogany table set for four people, now gathering dust in room number seven.

Monklè's hair has turned white and he occupies another room in the valley. Lola is finishing her secondary school years and preparing for the *baccalauréat* final exams. It is a credit to her and to her father's constant support that she got that far in her schooling—like the vast majority of Haitian children, she grew up speaking Kreyòl in an elite-culture-oriented educational system where they are taught in French.

Justin lusts after her and thinks it is love. He sees himself, her, and me as children of the same garden. He helps her with school and corrects her French grammar in her homework. When he sings his love for her, she laughs at him.

At night, before dragging his mattress to the plateau, Justin sits outside with Monklè and they talk. Years ago, the only time I ever happened to enter Monklè's room, I noticed he had a passport photo of me that he kept in the same large frame containing photos of his family.

CHORUS LAMENT

This morning again, the mourning dove came at my doorstep. She walks between the mint, basil, and pink geranium I keep in clay pots. Her head is soft and bare like a petal. The geranium has not bloomed yet.

Yesterday, on the stairs going down toward the plateau where Justin sleeps near his son's grave, I picked up a mourning dove's gray feather. I laid it in front of my father's photograph like one drops a solitary flower on a tombstone.

STAIRS

My father had a labyrinthine mind whose complex demands he partly solved by building stairs all over the land of his garden property. A differing god, Sunday was the day he did not rest and liked best for doing construction.

The stairs do not necessarily ascend. They crisscross the garden and curve like a snake's spine going toward many directions all at once.

While masons mixed mortar and hammered rocks into shapes that would enable them to follow a carefully set line of strings, my father watched over the building of his stairs like a general over a battlefield. He surveyed them like a map of secret war operations.

In this way, his Sunday prayer was about concrete form, foundations, direction, and permanence.

On those Sundays, Tonton was the black-angel mason who showed a gold tooth when he smiled. Sightings of Tonton's gold tooth were rare. Sweat streaked his cement-powdered chest with shiny black rivulets that ran and swerved past chalky nipples.

My father stood over him to observe the laying of every single stone. In the understanding each one had of the other man's concern for perfection, there was great respect.

I am now older than Tonton was when I thought him old. My father was silent a long moment and his eyes stared far in the distance when he learnt of Tonton's death.

"Tonton is an old fool who drank once too many. I warned him," he then said and bent his head down.

On Father's stairs Tonton taught me how to jump rope and never trip.

FATHER'S BACK

On those stairs, I remember Father's backside best. There, he is forever going up, turning his back on us, leaving us as we are—stairs left unfinished and without direction.

There was a red birthmark at the back of his neck, a little above the hairline. We only saw it when Father was fresh out of the barbershop.

He didn't turn around after I kissed him goodbye on the day he left me in a girls' boarding school in France. I watched the birthmark grow smaller while the distance between us grew bigger.

He didn't turn around when he left Justin in a boys' boarding school in Switzerland, and so he never saw how his twelve-year-old boy's face went pale, how his lower lip dropped and his eyes fogged. He didn't see his uncomprehending boy as he stood bravely, alone and skinny between dark, solid luggage. He didn't see him lean one skinny arm on a wall, rest his dolorous, adolescent face on the skinny arm, and shed tears that ran down that face, dropped on that skinny arm, colorless as the wall against which all this grief was projected.

He never saw that he treated us as if we were stairs—forms to be planned, controlled, shaped, directed, and leveled, spaces where he let big, hard stones drop to see them set in soft cement.

He didn't turn around, years later, as he walked away and up the stairs by the swimming pool after saying to me that after decades of doing it alone, it was my turn to take over the river valley rooms; he wasn't going to do it any more; let it all burn to hell, see if he cared.

PLAYING THE STAIRS

Time has made cracks in the stairs where the big *mabouya* lizards live. Their spotted gray skin matches the color of the aged cement.

As children, playing cowboys and Indians, we learnt from lizards how to chase after each other relentlessly up and down the stairs, to crawl slowly and hide in cracks. I nearly killed Justin with the metal-point arrows I got, with a bow to match, at Christmas time. Father had ordered toys for us from a U.S. catalog.

The rainy season would find Justin and me, naked as lizards, running down the stairs under pouring rain and jumping into the pool whose water felt warm in contrast.

These are stairs on which, in later years, each night, Alan came down to visit me in the poolside apartment where I was staying then, wearing his Japanese kimono and bringing me a marijuana joint.

The apartment was built under the pool terrace and had the same oval shape. During the day, I heard tenants over my head dragging the pool's wrought iron lounging chairs so they could get the best spot in the sun for themselves. During the night, it was the night watchman who dragged a chair so he could watch the moon instead of staying at his post by the gate.

Stairs where servants, now as they did then, go down with wash to do, come back up with ironed clothes set on hangers, go down with buckets to fill, come back up with mops and brooms.

Stairs to stand a moment to spot on the ground a fruit just heard falling—mango, breadfruit, or sour sap.

Stairs where Justin sat at night listening to the silence of trees, where he goes down at night carrying his mattress to sleep under God's face of stars, and where he climbs back up at dawn.

Stairs where I sat alone after Father's funeral and the night watchman came softly. "Hush, don't cry," he said. "Crying isn't good for you."

Stairs where last night, every night and as far back as I can remember, bald bats flew blind and low to bite the pool.

Stairs Bluet now runs up wearing a turquoise blue bathing suit, followed by her new dog, a golden dachshund she named Papaya, and where my own dog, Trotinette, used to follow me.

Bluet heads for the pool in her tits-free topless suit with a matching swimming cap that covers her blond hair with turquoise blue. She also wears a transparent, pale blue plastic visor through which she checks the sky when she reaches the pool and stands at the edge to take a dive. She opens her arms to find balance and get some élan. Then, she jumps as high as she can, holding her nose squeezed tight between two determined little fingers, and makes a shrill little squeak as she hits the water.

"Ah . . . how good it feels!" she says to Papaya when she resurfaces after the deep plunge, spurting water in between words.

Waiting for Bluet to emerge from under the water, Papaya had the same look in her eyes that Gigi had when, from the apartment window, she watched Betty taking a Sunday afternoon swim.

NATURE'S SPREAD

In the room I now occupy, I listen to sounds from the pool's small waterfall. In the daytime, it's dragonflies that kiss the surface of the pool lightly, in passing. But now that it is night, it's the bats' turn.

Inside, a gray fan sifts the air that reaches to my breast, naked above the brightly flowered bedsheets.

There are painted parrots in a painting on the right wall. They fly over a dense jungle through which a flowing brook runs between heart-shaped green and mottled-red malanga leaves.

On another wall, it is at zebras that I look. They stand in a lush flatland also divided by water. There are palm trees with red trunks, and in a delicate young-looking tree perches a chicken as big as the lion hidden in the tall grass below.

My face buried in the pillow, I want to forget about love. But thoughts are like smells, they reach you even when the doors are shut.

I try to remind myself that life is a turning wheel—something on the upside will undoubtedly happen.

Outside, Justin sleeps. He thinks himself a tree.

He habitually lies on his side, so half his face is turned up to the stars, the other half down to the earth like an Indian listening to its pulse.

His cheeks are the stage where two worlds meet.

One world above is that of poets when they write verse about the mystery of night, its lacework of foliage, the silence on the eyelids of birds, the lure of bright gems hung in the sky.

The other world is the world below, that of the depth-disturbed, the darkness-damned, and the dead.

Justin's son, buried underneath him, is a metaphor for the natural order gone wrong.

The earth is a vast skin that covers and hides its organs within. It conceals a body packed inside with life burdened with longings. It gives them form in roots, limestone, caves, boulders, tunnels, and pits. It spreads them through sap, oil, and sulfur pools. It sends messengers in the form of anything that can creep, crawl, bite, scratch, and infest. It is a body that absorbs and internalizes all of men's basements, men's underground lots, torture chambers, and atomic plants. It is a body that expresses a multilevel saga of screams through liquid substance that snakes and worms its way until it reaches a throat, a kind of narrowed point of release it holds as if with two clutching hands, then bleeds and vomits out of a volcano mouth. Through this mouth, it pours its own innards down the mountainside to denounce, dislodge, burn, and cover all of life outside that had until then dared express itself as crisp, clean, and coquette in lavish tapestries of greens and blues.

About sleeping under trees, Justin says, "It's paradise! You should see my dick at night. It stands straight to the stars."

Grande Jesula Gets a Visit

"Tita! Come here you dried up old cook! Get your face out of that chicken stew and bring the corn kernels to feed these pigeons before they start coming down on us and pestering this beautiful young lady who's here to see me.

"Already, she's come because of trouble with some dead bird that scared her. And the pigeons might spoil her dress. If that happens you won't have any ears left when I am done yelling at you and you won't hear your own screaming when the devil comes for you. Even these stupid pigeons notice how nice this child looks and they are curious . . .

"Come now, child . . . Don't be shy, don't mind me . . .

"And, Tita! Get that yellow dog with its tits dragging on my floor out of here! Stew or pigeons, I don't care what it's after. I am Mother of Spirits, not Mother of Dogs . . .

"Child, I am an old woman now but even when I was young I was never good-looking. But men found me very sexy . . . Now I still have two good eyes in that black face of mine. I know one of them looks askew—that one was operated on—but I can tell without a bit of hesitation that you are as pretty as if you were the last face God had a chance to make with His own hands.

"Aah yes, when He made you, God wanted to show off his art.

"You see me sitting on this temple's big old green straw chair in the middle of the dirt floor from morning to night like I am the president of Haiti giving audiences. But I am Mother of Spirits. I was never mother of a child. If I had been, that child would never have looked anything like you. And it's just as well I never had one because there are enough mothers running after ugly children and not nearly enough mothers to take care of all the Spirits.

"Besides, children leave us, whereas Spirits don't—they take care of us.

"I never chose to be Mother of the Gods. They chose me—everything I tried to do with my life when I was young, it all went wrong. Nothing worked out anywhere or with anyone. This went on until I obeyed them—they wanted me to build this temple and sit my forever-big ass where you see it today.

"You're not prissy about my language, are you? Me, I am not afraid of words or of anything. But . . .

"What's this! Shush! Shush! Damn pigeons are landing on me already? Food! Of course. They want food . . .

"Tita! Where did she go? Tita! Tita! Bring the corn for the pigeons! Damn it . . .

"Child, hand me that broom next to you . . . Yeah, this one . . .

"Shush! Shush!

"You can't be a Mother of Spirits if you've got no heart—you can't go to the cemetery to bargain with Baron Father of the Dead for someone he took away too soon—you won't have enough of your two legs to run when you start hearing his insults and his threats; he doesn't like to give back what he took; you won't outrun his escorts going after you, or escape from those hiding behind tombs, ready to catch you turning the corner.

"I was once in the Port-au-Prince cemetery and I stood my ground against a whole Society of Sanpwèl! I am sure you've heard how they are the most fearsome of the secret societies. Well, that night, either they had a deal to make with Death or they needed to dig out some poor soul already sold into zombie labor—they'd have had to get him before he woke up in his coffin.

"God as m'witness, that's the kind of magic I won't do—I don't do what's not done. No ma'am. Not me. And I didn't give in to the Sanpwèl either—I was there first; it was they who had to bow down to me.

"And bow down to me, they sure did.

"I don't do what's not done and that's why I can look Death in the eyes, any day, anywhere.

"It's not just anybody who can come inside my temple here and attend feast day rituals. I won't allow it. And I don't accept work just because someone can pay for it.

"Otherwise, I'd be rich. The walls here would get a fresh coat of paint and I'd get some better roofing than this corrugated iron stuff that piles up heat on top of my old head and keeps us sweating all day. The Spirits' rooms would get all dolled up too—I'd get them fresh paint, pink, new bedspreads, lace curtains, perfume, more rum and fresh flowers all the time.

"I'd even get help for Tita! You hear me Tita? If I were rich I'd get help for you—yes! I'd get help to help the help . . . Funny, isn't it?

"And just so I would not be surrounded by the mess of things you see on these rickety tables to my right and to my left—no more dusty fans, wood sticks, alarm clocks, sunglasses, toilet paper, pumpkins, shampoo, laundry soap, medicine and whatnot! I know what order is, but Tita does not.

"Tita thinks it's good to keep what you need close to you. She won't listen to me when I complain about it. She's a stubborn old goat.

"Still, I am going to have to clean up a bit before next month—I have an initiation coming up. The problem is, if I dust too early, I'll have to do it all over again right before the initiation. All these things to lift up! And each thing has a kind of tail because as soon as you move one thing you find something else that was hiding behind it . . . Anyway, I must be boring you with all that talk.

"Tita! Where is the corn? And I need a cigarette! Send for cigarettes at the corner store. These boys that stand around my front door all day trying to see what's going on in here, send out one of them, that'll give him something useful to do!

"And bring some iced water for the old man! Tita! Do you hear me?! Tita!

"He has been waiting for a good long bit . . . Tita! The old man is here! That's right . . . My friend, don't think I didn't see you when you came in a little while ago. Wait for me. I need to talk to you. I have to finish with this girl first. Just wait . . .

"But, child, you're letting me talk and talk . . . and I am only an ignorant old thing. What about that dead bird? A mourning dove you say? I hope you did not touch it.

"No? Good—because you don't know if it's an evil that was left there for you or if it is simply dead flesh that can carry disease.

"What? Ooh, you don't need to worry about that—doves die on their backs with their wings tucked all neatly anyway . . .

"What'd you say? Yes, even if it was pointed like an arrow at right angle to your door. Whatever it is, it is a minor thing, all considered. Nevertheless, we are going to check it in a moment. We'll go look at the cards in Èzili's room. She is a loving Spirit. I see well in that room.

"I hope you own your own place, even if it is, like you said, 'only a fourth floor apartment.'

"The question surprises you? Well, it shouldn't. These things are important—we are not birds; we need ground to stand on. When we are in love, we think we can fly. But birds get shot at, even though they fly high, minding their own—someone wants their wings, someone wants their meat, someone wants their love.

"What's that? Yes of course . . . there are birds of prey too.

"We have much in common with birds. With pigeons even. I watch the females that sit and wait. I watch the males who grab for anything you throw at them before they even know what it is.

"My grandmother gave me the land this house stands on. I could not afford to buy it now. I had done nothing for her and see what she left me. I think of all the people, all the men, dear God!

For whom I have done so much and sacrificed. They gave me nothing. Instead, they *took* from me.

"I hope, child, that you are not a stupid woman like I was. Because Spirits aren't going to help you—they want you for themselves, so they'll just watch you fall—they know you won't die from grief and you'll eventually come to them on your knees.

"But now, it is my turn to do for my grandmother. I was fooled by enough men to know which ones are no good and I don't waste my time on them any more.

"Every year, I make a feast for the dead. I don't have children, but . . . You have children?

"No? Why not?

"You can't have any? Ah, I see . . .

"You know, Tita likes to say that . . .

"But, where is Tita anyway? Tita! Tita! Where is the corn? Damn it . . . Where is that pouting nuisance of an old woman?

"She says that when she was a child, any nasty old dog could buy a piece of land around here. She is right. One must plan carefully . . .

"Old people know how much they have but not how much they have left.

"Look at my friend here, the old man . . .

"Shush! Shush! Shush, damn it! You birds think I am your tree? They are going to mess up my muumuu! It does look pretty though. Look at them: it's like the sky is breaking in a hundred pieces of wings, the way they come down on us. But they'll nip at anything until you notice and feed them!

"These pigeons are like children! Look at them. Except that they can't make us feel like we live anew the way children can.

"Lucky for them they don't worry about death all the time either. I wish we had the luck of pigeons—nobody throws corn for us—we have to feed ourselves. The only thing that comes down over me these days are pigeons and Spirits.

"OK, I admit . . . they are not the same . . . What'd you say? Company? You think they are company? But the pigeons don't even sleep here! Even though I built them these nests you see up there.

"You ask, where do they go? They go a couple of blocks from here under the high roof of the nunnery down the street . . . Yes, that's where they sleep! High up, no rent, no tax, and they leave the females behind to do the work sitting on the eggs. It's a swell life for them, right?

"And now look at these papers I get from the mailman: the mayor's office sent them. What nerve! I pay my property tax. I owe them nothing.

"The other day I went to prove it to them. I stuffed all my receipts under their noses. Still, today I get the same papers again.

"I should take Baron and his family of Gede Spirit there with me next time I go. Gede is death itself. My Dambala is far too polite. Gede do not mess around. Gede do not twist their mouths in a curl trying to get some French *tournure*: 'Voulez-vous, Monsieur, s'il vous plait, talk to me, s'il vous plait?'

"Nowadays there is no respect for old people. I do things straight. And I get this? Damn it!

"See the old man here? He is fed up too. I know why he came. These kinds of things are running him ragged till he is going to mess up his life good and soon.

"His wife died. He has property and he says, 'I can't stand to look at the place and I am going to sell it. I could use the money.'

"A place never did me wrong, it's people that do.

"So, he can't see *her* and he can't look at the place anymore either? Your love dies, and then what? You have to live anyway!

"Your love is not your life. Even alive and well at your side, your love can't watch over you.

"You sell, and then what? The money will go faster than the whole life it took you to get a place of your own. You can't come home to money. You can't lie down on money. You can't sit under the shade of a pile of money and smoke your pipe. You can't buy back half your place with all the money you'll get selling it.

"Again, just ask Tita and she'll tell you that when she was a child . . . But damn it! Tita! Where is that corn! Tita? Tita!

"The mayor's office can bug me with these notices. They can raise my blood pressure, but they can't rob me and they can't throw me out of here. But Tita says they don't need to throw me out with papers they send because it's the blood pressure they give me that'll kill me.

"She's been with me twenty years now and I am not dead yet. No sir.

"She watches me every morning. She says that I sprinkle sugar over my coffee like I am only baptizing it—same for salt. She laughs that I am careful about blood pressure and diabetes but that I know very well that they will get me in the end anyway.

"As far as dying is concerned, we're all going to die . . . Tita and me sooner than most . . .

"But I can't afford a stroke—I am already ugly. Can you imagine what I'll look like if I *do* a stroke?

"Ooh! Now here is the old man, leaving us . . . Hey! Old man! Can't you wait for me?

"No? Well OK, but listen to me while you're walking out of here anyway: when I die, I'll die on my own land, in my own place, in my own white sheets and not like some bird that falls anywhere in its flight—nobody knowing where you come from nor how to bury you. Land does not do you any harm. It's people that hurt you. Not a place. I don't have children to leave this place to, only Spirits. But, no matter. Strangers have been kinder to me than family. I have a will made out already—the Spirits cannot be put out in the streets. I am going but they are staying. I am Mother of Spirits. This is their place. And I'll tell you one more thing: it's people like you that will make us lose everything. Go ahead and sell the land! Sell everything to the first stranger. These days, they come from all over with their foreign money. You find them all over town and all along John Brown Avenue where they wait for you to trade all that's yours for their 'greenback.' Pretty soon, we won't have any land to stand on and we'll have no country to call our own. No land. No roots. Nobody. Nothing. Go then. Go. I won't care . . .

"Now, child, let's see about your problem. Let's go read what the cards have to say about you. Let's go to Èzili's room.

"We don't have much time because I need to have my hair done. My boyfriend is coming back in a couple of days . . .

"But these pigeons are getting on my nerves. See how they pace? I don't know what has come over Tita!

"It is the one thing that bothers me about this getting old: white hair. It itches.

"You can't see it under my blue scarf but it's there nonetheless. I must get rid of it before he comes. You see, my boyfriend is forty and I'll be seventy-one, next month! Yeah!

"I can see by your face you have the 'what about the age difference' look. Well, one of us has to be older, right? And it's me. So what?

"And yes, I know what you are thinking . . . Everybody does . . . 'And what about children? Someday he'll want a younger woman and to have children' . . . You won't live if you worry about all there is to worry about!

"Look, my boyfriend did want to have a child. Like the rest of us, he wants to see his face in a child that will live on beyond him, see his parents' faces—he wants to live forever!

"I can't tell him that it does not work. I can't tell him that a child cannot extend his life—your own life on earth is all the time you get.

"He is a young man and illusions belong to the young. Anyway, I guess he'd have company at least. He might be less afraid, maybe . . . And I did let him go for a few months. Yes, that's right. I did. And no, I don't like to share my man any more than you would. No woman does.

"I see that these things are on your mind . . . yes?

"So, he had a child with someone. Afterwards, he came back to me. Now he has that child. He is satisfied. So what?

"The hurt? You ask about the hurt. What hurt? If I hurt, I keep that inside.

"I'm not going to die because of a man. My heart may love you but it won't allow you to destroy or disrespect me. There're some words I won't let a man get away with. I'll slash him instead. And I can't take stinginess either. Tight fingers and keeping accounts— small minds! If your heart feels big for me, it's got to show it big, like land does at the harvest.

"But come on up. Follow me to Èzili's room. I talk too much and time's passing fast.

"What's that? You think having a child with another woman is disrespect? Why? Let him have a baby! But let him take care of it too! Every man slips once in a while. You won't live if you worry about such stuff. Hold on to what you have. Life slips out easily enough all by itself. Didn't you hear what I told the old man earlier? You can't leave a man because of some whore. Let out the whore in you instead. Give him something he can't get anywhere else.

"OK, now. Remove your shoes before you enter Èzili's room . . . Hold that clay jar . . . Pour water from it three times and then you make your request.

"Aie! Watch yourself! Aie!

"Why did you startle like that?

"A spider? So what? It's nothing—just an *anasi* spider. The anasi is Èzili's. And now you've dropped the jar on its account.

"Yes, I know you're sorry . . . Anyway, no problem. This means she likes you. She may have already answered you in this way. She rules over love.

"We need to check about your love.

"You have a boyfriend?

"Yes? We'll see about him.

"Come in. Watch for the palm hanging from the ceiling.

"Sit. No, no! Not there, not by the altar. Come over here instead.

"Now, pick up that low chair and sit in front of me.

"Put the *laye* tray on your knees and shuffle the cards.

"Good! Well done. Now, choose one.

"Ooh! The Immaculate Conception: that's you! You really are Èzili's child!

"Let's see what else . . . You dream of snakes?

"Yes? And your head is like an ocean, is it? Yes! The spirit of the ocean loves you . . . You will live by the sea someday.

"Shuffle the cards again and pick three.

"Ooh . . . I see who sent the dead bird . . . the oldest trouble in the world . . .

"Don't worry. This is what I want you to do: tonight, you light three candles on the floor. Arrange them in a triangle facing east or north. Place a glass of sugar water in the middle of the triangle. Stand and pray. Call out to all your Spirits—those on your mother's side and those on your father's side. Tell them your hopes. Tell them what you want. When the candles have burnt down to the middle, pour three drops of the sugar water on the floor and then take a sip. Blow off one candle and put it under your pillow. Let the other two burn out. Leave the water near your head while you sleep.

"What did you say? 'Afraid to forget'? Now, what's there a mind can't remember! Just listen: in the morning, before you say a word, take a sip of the sugar water; in the evening, light the candle that was under your pillow and let it burn itself out. If you dream, come and tell me. I'll know what to do.

"Remember: trouble is only a situation in search of a solution. Sorrow is a worldview.

"What? You want to know if I know about the bird? Yes . . . I know about the bird . . . The bird is your love. Your love's a dead bird. Your man may be a learned man but he's got no head. At least, none other than what's between his legs . . . A man like that is easy to get, easy to lose. The wind knows its own mind better than this man does.

"But let's close now. You need to go and I need to do my hair.

"Watch your step! Don't start fainting on me . . . Steady . . .

"Hold on to your head, child. Listen, a man is just a man and there are no diamonds on any dick. Your own life is what's most precious.

"And watch that your feet don't get hurt on those clay shards . . .

"Ooh! And who do I see coming, finally? Here is our Tita! And so, Tita? Where is the corn I have been asking for?

"What? Get it myself? You quit! What? But that's absurd!

"Not absurd? You've been with me for twenty years! I have been putting up with you for twenty whole years, your lousy cooking, your mess all over, your deaf ears, your sullen moods, and when you need me now the most and have nowhere to go, and will find no one that will hire some washed-up old hag like you, you quit?! And no notice?

"What did you say? I don't deserve any?

"No? Not one thought for me, also an old woman, you leave me on the spot with no other help around? And you do this in front of my visitor? You want to shame me?

"What'd you say? It's you I shame?

"Go then, go! Shush! Shush! Out you go! No better than pigeons—no gratitude! No loyalty! Shush!

"Now I know why Spirits wanted me to keep pigeons—it's not for company, it's for reminder.

"Child, now listen. I know you are hurting. And you don't know what to believe in all I said. I am playing down your hurt because it's best for you. I know that what I saw is right, I am sorry to say. Of course, you need to find that out for yourself.

"The bird is not harm. It's just a message.

"Remember me when you learn the truth; when you find that what you thought was your own really never was; when you see that the people you trusted have become strangers; when you accept that the man you thought was yours has knocked up some young blond thing.

"Remember me because a woman's pain is every woman's pain. We may seem like different people but we are alike in destiny.

"Understand that when people have the least heart, they also make the least sense in the way they act. So don't even try to sort it out.

"What is sordid is not worth understanding.

"Stand your ground, child. Don't sell yourself short. Shush away the people who hurt you like you do pigeons—SHUSH!

"And TITA! Get your ass over here!

"I've got to talk to you or else you don't know what hell is going to open if you leave! How dare you play some dirty trick on me like that!

"Get on with your work! I am not Grande Jesula, Mother of Spirits, for nothing!

"If you haven't learnt who I am, it's high time you do. DAMN IT!"

The Chapel

I am a chapel. A simple white pentagon of rough-cast cement blocks aired through two wooden doors and cedar shutters. The past haunts and decorates me. The present crosses me from one door to the other like someone running after a second chance. The future takes its cues from the sky. Over the mountain ridge in the near distance, clouds emerge, mist and light, in patterns reminiscent of smoke messages the likes of which one might fantasize were sent by Caribs, first inhabitants of our Haiti. When the evening comes, God's face then is a night-full of stars that lay to rest on the nearby tadpole water.

It rained a short while ago. A loud tropical downpour the way I love them. Sometimes, I hear its gallop first, coming down the mountain. Then, progressively, rain is like drapes being pulled from tree to tree. Behind its stage curtain, nature rehearses this stock piece: the earth's cells become engorged with water; holes darken; great succulent plants bow their wide-leafed heads to camouflage and store deep green belly laughs; mahogany trees bend long blackened necks; drums are at my doors; cymbals percolate on my rooftop.

Rain stops as suddenly as it starts. Maestro made a final gesture. But silence rumbles still. The stream running below the garden terraces has swollen immensely. Water Spirits who inhabit me want to be revered and their hopeful sighs ripple through my blood.

My ears are attuned to every life murmur in this great park where the one who built me only planted fruit-bearing trees, besides mahogany. Everything breathes in a heavy, moist smell of moss musk. It is the time when dizzied breadfruits will let go of the branch and the thud on my roof vibrates inside me like an ill bee.

It is then too that roosters feel they must announce the end of rain. Here, they'll kick up a din for any occasion. It is much too joyful a feeling, this throat-full of shrill, to be let out just for the once-a-day-at-dawn affair. Afterward, dogs think they must respond with a throat-full of bark. And so it goes on with no respite, this back and forth banter, because here, island territory, it would seem that roosters don't sleep at night, though they perch. Dogs neither sleep nor perch. They are tied down somewhere in the nearby slums whose gray fossils' framework hangs amidst bushes at the foot of the mountain. It is as if everything is held, somehow, at the foot of something greater, be it dogs, slums, people, or me. I lie at the foot of the one I love.

Late afternoon is the time when she comes to visit. The time when woodpeckers return their russet heads to the home-holes stacked up in a straight line they dig for themselves into palm tree trunks. And while parrots are having their nonsense riot in high branches, the same woodpeckers will then peek out of their holes, fly out to some close by tree, and cackle breathlessly. Up and down and around the *kayimit* tree, lizards have a game of tag which they stop now and then only to swell their throats as if to gloat over their feats of gravity.

They scatter their free-running fun in defiant contrast to heavy-loaded and humorless ants working in two opposite streams of industrious lines. *Vingt-quatre-heures*—black-bodied, red-winged, bee-size flying devils whose sting children believe will kill you in twenty-four hours—like to buzz over the carpet of dry leaves where iguanas prowl. And, hidden beneath the purple underside of *malangas* whose large, heart-shaped leaves proliferate around the vanilla-scented spring, I know there is a rat.

You can tell I love this place! Specially when she comes to visit the garden, she whom I love as if she were part of me, daughter of the man who built me here.

She sits on the garden steps and lets her eyes float into me—God my heart, God my horizon, God much too vast for one to capture between two hands in a dream and so one looks for a being of flesh to whom to tell words of love. The same words she used to tell him when he lived here: "You are my chapel."

He was a foreigner, almost an old man already, an astrologer whom many people came to consult but that no one befriended.

"Haiti," he told her, "is the mystical island. It is my destiny."

His solitude preoccupied no one because he seemed so full of what everyone thought they lacked—knowledge about the direction and meaning of life.

How could he feel lonely if planets surround his heart and families of the sky uphold him?

Yet I know that, sometimes, just the open door was a painful sight to him—like a ready welcome to no one, a reminder of his aloneness in a house peopled by the thin-air bodies of invisible beings that spoke to him but never touched him.

He had wanted to find the magic place where perhaps God Himself would be awaiting him, and also a place where the beauty of the garden was not marred by memories unclear, undesired, unkind. Yet, the unspoiled clarity of the landscape he had wished for actually carried more emptiness than he could bear.

He discovered instead how alone he stood in the distance that separated him from the God he had hoped to find.

So, when open doors and windows showed him the desolate vastness of this new world rather than his place in it, he would withdraw to the vastness in him that was filled with familiar feelings and the display of memory's *trompes l'oeils.*

At those times when he would shut all doors and windows, lock himself in with incense and the music of his birthplace, it would seem to neighbors that these gestures were meant to keep the world out when actually it was to forget how outside the world he felt and was.

After he died, she came to live here—in me—as well, only for a short while until her life took her far away from us, far away from our story. People had thought it macabre that she'd want to come and live here where he had died. But instead, she saw me as the place where he had lived.

"There can be no better place to live than the chapel—the place most suited to remember him, an emblematic site," she said to friends.

On her second day here, she opened wide the door of the large cage where he had kept mourning doves. They hesitated a long while before taking this chance to fly away. She let them go less out of noble feelings about freedom than out of the desire to be relieved of their mournful cries.

Her father brought her four parrots to replace the doves—he did not see the joy of an empty cage. The parrots' early dawn cackles and shrieks jolted her out of bed and she grew to both need and resent their lively spirit.

She eventually realized that he was no longer here to be found either and that all that lingered here from him were just dream traces—her own. In the course of many months, she kept company with those traces and used them to imagine herself back to a kind of inner quiet and reconstruct the sense of her own being as reason enough to live.

The air was no longer a carrier for incense as it had been. It was allowed to be tainted only by heavy fragrances and subtle changes of tropical seasons. The sudden yellow outbreak of butterflies at the time of the yearly feast of Saint John became a season in itself. When the butterflies died out, she left.

Words from the Apocalypse I often heard him read out loud came back to me: *The light of the lamp will no longer shine in your house, and the voices of the husband and of the wife will no longer be heard there.*

The first morning after he had died and his body had been taken away, she lay facedown on the cold mosaic floor with arms open like a penitent. She did not cry, she screamed. She felt as if the damnation, curse, and abandonment of the whole human race weighed on her soul. (*But the earth came to rescue the woman; it opened its mouth.*) Yet, discomfort from the hard floor eventually forced her to get up and shift away from her despair. Giving in to the body can be a saving kind of humility.

Since she has left, the garden has come to a different rhythm, paced by the careful cadence of worm-seeking hens and their yellow chicks, the brisk outburst of mahogany nuts and *tchatcha* seeds, the crack of lightning, the dim thump to the ground of ripened mangoes hollowed by birds and rats. And the rain.

But for me, it is as if I live solely in her thoughts—no one else since has gone through my doors nor opened the cedar shutters. In her heart she carries my image, indivisible from memories of him.

Because she does not forget, she is the country where I live, the lungs that lend me breath, the island that defines my shores. Lodged in her, I transform as she transforms, I know all that she knows as she knows it. Her lamp, if she lights it, will be mine.

We are again quite alone when she is back to visit the garden. She sits here, and in a way too, I sit in her.

At those times when she remembers him most vividly, his favorite quotes from the Bible, like parentheses in a book of dreams, present themselves in my head with a peculiar resonance. (*Listen, I have chosen you. Carry out the prayer so you remember me.*)

When she remembers him, she first sees images of him in her mind's eye. What she did not actually see when he lived seems clearer in her mind, truer to who he was, more real than what he presented to her as himself, even though he loved her.

So she sees him put on all white clothes (*And to him was given fine linen to wear, shining and pure; because fine linen stands for the just work of Saints*), and then she sees him take a knife, the sharpest—he intends to kill the sheep with one sweep—because the animal must not suffer. Pain hardens the heart and spoils the meat.

To most who met him, he seemed a brusque, private man. From his experience of life, he had always kept something like the feeling of stone on bare back. (*Those who wear white robes are those who come from great troubles.*) He came to believe his heart had been lost as well, until she appeared at his door for a reading of the future.

When he first met her, he was unprepared for what he said to be "just a broken bird, dear God!"

But she sees him in dismembered ways, so the prayer is important—it carries him back to her in a meaningful sequence. She sits on the steps. The mountain is ahead of her with clouds lighting old smoke signals she read as a child, sitting on the same steps. She never forgets the mountain because the signals from childhood weigh inside her. At times, she feels like she is an offering that awaits the knife—times when there is so much to give and no one in front of whom to stretch it all.

So she wonders if the inner sense of waste in her is from the blood that has already emptied from the flesh. Perhaps this is the reason why the sequence of her remembering starts with an offering (*I have placed in front of you an open door that no one can shut*)—after he has killed the sheep, she sees him rinse the blood from the knife under the tap outside my western door.

By then, the charcoal has reddened.

While the meat cooks, he lowers all the shutters, closes both doors, locks himself in, puts music on—the chants and drums he liked to record during Vodou ceremonies he attended throughout the countryside. She knows he danced, forgetting the meat over the charcoal, until he was as dizzy and sodden as the rain-soaked breadfruits that drop on my roof.

"Spirits wanted some," he'd say, and, smiling to himself, scatter the burnt pieces around the garden.

After he had done the first astrological reading for her, she had asked him for his own date of birth. On that date, she came to see him with a cake.

"No one has ever brought me a birthday cake," he said as he took it, and forgot to offer her a slice.

She would have only liked to sing for him. She mumbled her birthday wishes and left. He used to say about himself that the solitude of the astrologer is in the image of John the Baptist's, sent ahead of us to level the way for God—*He is the voice of the one who cries in the desert.*

Now that he is gone, she feels his voice in her own.

"Your territory is that of an arid mountain," he had said to her. "Free yourself from all that is superfluous." (*The two wings of the big eagle were given to the woman so she could fly to the desert, to her own place where she is fed for a while.*)

He showed her how to pray—he knelt to the ground and raised his arms open: "*Oh my people! Enter the holy land for which God destined you!*"

She came back regularly to see him at prayer time, smelling of fresh soap. Soon however, too soon, she found she was praying for him rather than with him. She knelt on the rug he'd woven for her. He had dyed the wool himself, with leaves and bark gathered from this land where she was born, daughter of the man who built me so that I could give her shelter and a home.

To her first visits, she came with the complaint that her life "lacked horizon."

"*The fruits your soul desired went far from you,*" he quoted to her, by way of welcome—he knew that by giving a larger spiritual frame to her visit, he would ease her timidity.

She grew accustomed to his speaking in quotes.

Speaking in quotes was his way of showing that every human act decided on, each experience undergone, is understood through every holy book of every age and culture as being more meaningful, having broader scope, than it appears at first glance. It was his way of revealing how these seemingly banal human acts are in fact connected to a larger design of significant, repeated patterns, a kind of unconscious undercurrent that, unawares, leads us to the understanding of the very reason for our existence and of what happens to us in it.

She always felt new breath after he had "opened the sky for her," as he would say. She did not see how, nor when, she grew to love him, because it seemed the love was always there.

———

To explain himself, he once told her that *"the one who emigrates onto God's ways will, on earth, find numerous possibilities and spaces."*

She knew that in his youth, in the ways of the prophets he tried to emulate, he had left his birthplace and the religion in which his parents raised him. (*Do no harm to the earth, to the sea, nor to the trees, until we have marked the foreheads of God's servants.*)

"In my youth," he said, "I dreamt that one day I would manage to kill all base instincts so that in a new, serene climate, the migrating people of my soul might visit the great temples and climb onto celestial territories."

Yet, it is here, on her land, in her garden, that she found him, in his old age, in me, the chapel.

She was too young to understand that she was young. She was young enough not to see that she was too young, yet old enough to know it did not matter.

———

The chapel came to house illness. He was to give his last breath in her presence. The lungs were ill. Breathing became dark and strenuous. The sky had shifted. The chapel was drifting. He refused to see any doctor, or receive any care.

"I want to die all in one piece."

Once he had become ill, she came here each morning and left early evening. On what turned out to be the last night of his life she had somehow refused to leave in spite of his insistence that she should.

Rising! Floods! Deluge! He sees he is Noah who appears on the ark's deck and water covers the earth. Noah has broken all moorings with this world of illusions and sails on uncertain currents, but trusts in God's will.

Separated by a curtain, he laid in bed as she sat on a mattress stretched over the bare floor. (*Let us watch over one another so love gets stirred.*) He had pulled the curtain himself—he was always a man of great modesty. Waiting for death, struggling for breath and battling with fear, he felt more naked than ever before. When she, unawares, was dozing off in the early hours of dawn, it was not Noah she heard, but him, whispering in what she now knows was his last breath.

"*God, make me land in a blessed place; in truth, it is you, the sweetest of places.*"

To allow the sequence of remembrance its own design, she tries to stand pure and free of all images or forms, the way she thinks God wishes us to be.

They had known each other for only a short while, yet enough to last for what she imagined eternity could be. (*He will live with them. . . . He will wipe all tears from their eyes, and death will no longer exist; there will no longer be mourning, nor cries, nor pain.*)

To remember him is to let his voice come, hear it when he sat at his work table and closed his eyes before speaking, as if truly he was addressing someone absent. (*His face was like the sun when it shines in full strength.*) She wondered if this was a kind of death—the way he erased himself, serving as a mirror to reflect the stars' will, in the hope of easing the anxiety for the future which had come to his doorstep in the heart of a stranger.

To remember him is to smell incense—myrrh and amber! It is to see him walking with sandals along the garden's terraces, gathering leaves and tree bark he'll use to color wool. Later, when he pulls the wool from large cooking pots full of boiling water, he'll marvel and delight in the subtle hues that came out.

"Die before you die," he said—an advice for her to remember.

And the image that now comes up in the sequence is that of his naked body pulled out of a drawer at the morgue.

"I do not want to go to the morgue. This kind of place is impure. Bury me straight away. Right in the earth. Plant a tree," he asked.

Before she understood either how it happened or that she could not have prevented it, he did end up at the morgue. And there she followed him, to prepare his body for burial. (*The body washed with water that is pure.*) But when she stood in front of his nude corpse, she remembered his modesty.

It was just the day before that, in the silence of the early morning, she had pulled open the white curtains behind which he had hidden his dying and saw what she was unprepared for. She saw he was dead.

The Lord is close to those whose hearts are breaking.

She realized she had not understood what had been happening all these past few days. Her lagging awareness had kept her in a time far behind the reality and time in which he lived during his dying—Time had already separated them long before he died.

If Time is ahead, one could believe it possible to run after it and catch up. But Space, you can't run after. Seeing him dead she gasped at the sense of the gap, the expanse, the void, and the cosmic emptiness that now would keep them ever separate and unattainable to each other.

Could she catch up on that Space, that Immensity, she thought, if she learned to die before she died?

How not to fear death when one must witness and suffer the way people behave toward it and handle the remains?

She rented space in a private grave at the Port-au-Prince cemetery. Death as a farce with painted puppets has to stage its development in immured cells. Mortification and trial, until, *Lazarus! Rise! Come out of your grave!* When a year had passed, she went to get him out of the cemetery. Reclaim him.

The dilapidated and weed-choked downtown Port-au-Prince cemetery was given over to goats and homeless mendicants. The guardian at the gate let her drive in without so much as a glance—one cannot watch over the Dead; they watch us. The living cannot arbitrate what goes on in these dwellings. The Dead alone can govern there and let happen what must. So please, go ahead! Go face them; they know your heart. (*Here, I come, oh God, to accomplish your will.*)

Sitting on top of a grave in the otherwise deserted cemetery she found an idle adolescent boy who needed a little money. So, to remember him, early dawn, with pickax and shovel, they opened the grave, pulled out the coffin, lifted the lid, and carried him out.

She holds it in her hands—a little bit of paper, folded for so long it is breaking at the creases. Just a note, one among the many he had sent her—words scribbled in haste with a pencil though he had mulled them over a long time beforehand. From the steps where she sits, dazed by memories, she unfolds the note and reads it aloud:

"What is there to fear when you are my companion, and, while in absence, you remain my confidante?"

His retrieved body was to stay in me, the chapel, for three days, wrapped in the same white cloth in which he had been laid in his coffin. Deposed so on the bed, he seemed reduced to a small unnecessary bundle. The only substance, the only weight left, was the love. (Zachary had cried: "*Shout for joy, daughter of Zion, because here, I have come, I will live with you.*")

She succeeded in finding a new burial place for him in the high mountains of Seguin, on land owned by a friend who agreed to let her dig a grave.

"I know he will like it there," she said to me, "to walk among pine trees, no longer feeling hot and ill as he was here. At dawn, there is a soft fog more like mist! Dew covers the grass and his sandals will take in the dampness."

With his beloved music playing through the loudspeakers on the day she set off with his body to the mountains of Seguin, how he must have danced! His soul and the music, enchanted with each other, free, swirling loose, and drifting like incense through the cedar shutters, the day she set off to his final resting place with his remains.

Much later, after she had buried him this second time, she heard that people in Seguin say they sometimes see a ghost in the early morning mist.

"It is like an aurora," they try to describe. "The light of his being is profiled on celestial light—it is light on light." (*My angel will walk ahead of you. Watch him because he bears my name.*)

The sequence is running short and, still sitting on the steps, she closes her eyes to bring him back some more. Loving him has taught her the preciousness of bundles that weigh in the mind—unwrap them carefully lest the contents spill fast like dust.

Yet unwrap them knowing what's inside flows like water and must not be held onto. And like Moses's mother about to abandon him to the Nile, she will hear God's words:

Don't be afraid. Let him fall. Because I have let my love fall on you and on him.

Venant
Found
It Hard
to Know

"Listen, this happened in our very own Haiti! As real as my name is Venant, there he was—Papa Gede! Standing in his specially-reserved-for-him black redingote and saying, That goat is missing a piece so I'm not taking it! Then he stomped and grinned. The *oungan* who was officiating called all the *ounsi* and told them to stop dancing so they could come and help him plead with that Spirit who just showed up and took over somebody's whole mind so he could act out on this earth for a little while. The music stopped, the ceremony stopped, nobody's talking, even the goat's not breathing. I must say however that the rope was really tight around its neck—if it moved, it choked—so forget about being able to run away if that's what it had in mind, and it must have, unless it had no sense. Because, for the goat, this was a life-and-death situation though it had no say in this matter of how it lives or when it dies. Anyway, this oungan, a big man-chunk kind of a priest, had gotten all the ounsi on their knees in front of Papa Gede, and was telling Papa Gede they bought that goat with all the money they had, chose the best there was, it's now the middle of the night, there's no time, or money, to get another, and then too, Goat had been washed, dressed, it ate the tester food in the plate—Goat agrees to be offered—and was standing there quietly for Papa Gede to take him. Take him? For Goat, that meant getting cooked. Literally. But Papa Gede stomped again, yelling that the goat is missing a piece and he's NOT taking it. Then, he almost stepped on the oungan on his way to the other side of the room where he could get closer to and flash his eyes at everybody standing there watching the scene. Nobody was talking, even the children, and my brother's new baby stopped sucking at his mother's nipple. Me, I was holding the giggles so hard, I peed in my panties. You'd think Papa Gede knew it since he stopped right in front of me and eyed me down from behind the sunglasses he likes and that are handed to him when he shows up in a ceremony, and all I could see was only that one left eye of his because, as always, he had that one lens taken out. So, there was Papa Gede standing in front of me and I was pinching myself because Papa Gede's face was my little sister's face. My sister was glaring at me—that night Papa Gede possessed my sister! And there she was, so completely overtaken by the Spirit she didn't know she was standing in front of me, her big sister, soaked in my own pee I was trying so hard not to laugh because Papa Gede didn't think it was funny the rope around Goat's neck was so tight it had rubbed off a little bit of the skin and because of that he found Goat was no longer presentable, offerable that is, and he was not gonna take it like that, not until he's got us all dragged on our knees long enough begging him to please, ooh please, take it now since it's midnight, the ceremony has started, the food's on the table, the hot pepper liquor's on the table, the calabash bowls are filled, the drums are warm, tight, and ready, the ounsi are all in their white dresses, even me, with Papa Gede eyeing me down, daring me to laugh if I dare.

"For this, I had come home? This was happening at my family home where we all grew up. The ceremony was for my sisters, my brothers, and me. I am a *dosou*. Now, dosou is the child born after twins—Clotilde and Clovis were born before me. But also, *dosa* is the child born before twins. And you see, I am a dosou and a dosa because Jocelyne and Jocelin who are also twins were born after me. Even though twins are really powerful, I am the one with the most power because I was born between two sets of twins. Everybody has been saying I should become a *manbo* and take care of the Spirits because my head is full of them and God knows how they dance in there! But now, I am *levanjil*—a Gospel-head—I am a convert, I am a Protestant. That's a problem here—the Spirits say they'll have me begging in the streets for betraying them. There are days when it looks like they'll win, days when they have me under their control, days like when I was sick in bed with a foot so swollen-big it didn't look like it belonged to my body, a foot so sore it couldn't touch even the bedsheet, couldn't rest on the mattress. I have a neighbor who knows how to use herbs and roots. She cures everybody, but me, she couldn't help. Heaven help me if she didn't try! And that same night she had a dream where an old man with a stick was running after her yelling, You better disappear, you better disappear right now or I'll fix your own foot too! In the morning she came to warn me that my kind of illness was just not her 'department'; my illness was spiritual—Spirits had ahold of me—and Jo, my husband, had better find an oungan who could do something about that foot. My husband brought someone that same afternoon. The minute this man lays his eyes on me he says it's the Marasa, it's the Twin Spirits that are holding me—they are mad at me, this foot thing is a threat like they are telling me I ain't free to walk over to the Protestants, I better respect them, I better have a ceremony for them, I better feed them, in fact I better organize a whole Manje Lwa feast for all the family's Spirits. So that night, Jo lit five candles to make a promise, for me, for Clotilde and Clovis, for Jocelyne and Jocelin.

"Now you need to understand that Jo is levanjil too. And he's been fighting against his own Spirits who dance in his head like they do in mine but a lot worse—in his head it's Mardi Gras all the time. Jo can't find any peace from all that Spirit-drumming-in-the-head kind of thing, wherever he is: never mind if Jo is sitting on a church bench and a Bible is sitting in the palms of his hands, still, clear as can be, he sees a Spirit who comes to ask him, What the hell do you think you are doing sitting in a church? And mind you, he is not sleeping when he sees them—his eyes are peeled wide-open as they can ever be! Another time, again in church, imagine him sitting in his own peaceful-sitting way and he suddenly hears a voice whispering in his ears, Go and buy two lottery tickets for number 28 and its reverse 82, do it NOW! Well of course, Jo immediately shuts Bible-and-all and runs to buy the lottery. And what do you think happened if it's not 28 that comes out first and 82 second?! It's with that money we were able to pay the accounting school's tuitions for our eldest boy. Jo *cannot* be levanjil. Every time he tries to pray, every time he gets caught singing hymns, he spends the whole night without being able to sleep because of all the Spirits caroling in his brain. So, you see, this is the same Jo who lit five candles for us Marasa, Dosou and Dosa. This is my Jo.

"Spirits announced to my family that I would show up at ten. I was coming all the way from Port-au-Prince and at ten o'clock sharp I pushed the wooden gate open, I entered my home. All the offerings were set, all dishes displayed. That reminded me of the time when I was five years old and the five of us were sitting on the ground under the tamarind tree, each one with a small calabash bowl set in front of us full of food because my father was doing a Manje Lwa for Marasa. I checked into my calabash: I didn't see any pig's ears and no mouth either—my favorites! I went to look for those ears and mouth in the big pot of food that was still cooking. I saw none. Some devil took ahold of me and I stuck my finger in the middle of the food and all the food got spoiled—remember, I am a dosa, I am powerful and my anger works like a devil's. My father asked me, What do you want? I showed him my fist—that means I want a bull. If I had wanted a goat I would have shown three fingers. If it had been a chicken I wanted I'd have shown one finger. One year later my father did sacrifice a bull and the five of us were again sitting under the tamarind tree, a full calabash between our legs. Mine had the ears, the mouth, and best of all, the eyes!

"You don't mess with a dosa, but mostly, you don't mess with Spirits. I knew better and I shouldn't have allowed myself to end up stuck in bed with a big foot. I know what I am supposed to do. I always know what's going to happen just like I did when I was pregnant with Marie-Ange: I was sitting under the tamarind tree and a Spirit took possession of Clotilde who came and stood in front of me, looked at my pregnant belly, and asked, Does this house only shell out girls? That's how the Spirit in Clotilde told me I was carrying a girl and, what's more, also what name to give her. I know I am supposed to be a manbo and be a mother of Spirits. I know I am also supposed to marry a Spirit and buy him a ring. Yet I married Jo. I was wearing his ring and not the Spirit's. I lost the ring. Why do you think I lost that ring? Spirits! That's why. Jo bought me a second ring. How do you think I lost it too? Spirits! Same thing happened to Jocelyne when she got engaged: Moutcho Woulo, a family Spirit, wanted her to wear a ring for him and she didn't do it. She got engaged and they made plans to marry in June. June goes by and no wedding. July goes by, no wedding. October goes by! No wedding still. Whatever they do, something comes to ruin their plans. So Jocelyne bought the ring for Moutcho Woulo and she wears it. Next week, the wedding was on. What d'you think of that?

"So finally, I was at the gate. But you know, to start with, the twins had said they couldn't wait for me and had organized the Manje Lwa one week earlier than the time I could come home— all the food got spoiled. And I hadn't even been there to stick my finger into anything. You'd think they would have remembered what happened when I was five? Plus they prepared all the wrong stuff, like they were supposed to buy a *pentle* chicken and they bought a *zenga* chicken. Imagine! And it was like that for every single food item. The Spirits messed it all up in their heads so they would have to wait for me. And now, here was DOSOU-DOSA! At the gate and happy to be home 'as a pig is in shit.' There was a table spread specially for the Marasa—*tchaka*, candy, cakes, soft drinks, and all the foods they like. But there was food also for all the family Spirits: we had for Ti Jan, for Papiyon, for Èzili also, with her perfume bottle set on her very own chair. We had for Moutcho Woulo too. We had roasted food for Legba—roasted plantain, yam, sweet potato, corn. We had beef cooked in sauce for our Ogou the way he likes it and roasted goat for our Feray. We had a table for the Dead that was laid out with pumpkin soup, coffee, cassava, peanuts, roasted corn. And we had for Papa Gede too! That goat-with-a-piece-missing-so-he-won't-take-it kinda goat, among other good, good food!

"But who do you think I found lying down sick on a mat in the middle of the Spirits' sacred room? Had been like that all morning, in spite of all the good, good food, in spite of the drums, the morning breeze, the morning sun rays, and moaning her lungs away, crying for me? Jocelyne! And everybody was waiting for me to make her well. WELL!? But what was wrong with her? I told them flatly I am no doctor and besides, nobody's ill here, there is no illness here, nothing is wrong with Jocelyne. And after that, who do you think was the one who suddenly gets up with a grin? That same grin Papa Gede had on his face at midnight after he said there is a piece missing on the goat and he won't take it? Yes, Jocelyne! And who do you think got possessed by one Spirit after another all day long, relentless, repentless, here and there, grinning? Yes, the same one that ended up planted in front of me after having refused to take the goat that was missing a piece, and was eyeing me down with that one-eyed pair of sunglasses, daring me to laugh if I dare. I tell it now, and I'll probably tell it always: no matter how much you know what you are supposed to do in life, it's still hard to know."

Dame Marie

On the morning I was leaving Port-au-Prince for
Dame Marie, stopping through Jeremie, a mourning dove paused
an instant below my window, and when it flew away, it dropped
an underbelly feather that descended to the ground calmly like a
large snowflake.

It was hot in the plane, so small that we had to bend down to
get in and take our seats. During all of takeoff and a good while
afterward, a red rooster in a cage stacked in the back with luggage
kept screaming for glory, for the thrill, for the torment. The pilot
smiled each time he heard it.

The singing of the rooster, however, made me think of the
sounding of the bugle that I imagined Gustave heard so strongly

in his heart when, in New York, he made the decision to change the course of his life—perhaps he hoped to change that of his countrymen as well—by joining the rebel groups. He must have heard it also when he said farewell to his family, over the phone with some, or over coffee as he did with Uncle Edward who tried to dissuade him.

The sound of the bugle must have been present still when he disembarked at night with his companions on the white beach at Petite Rivière de Dame Marie; also present when he saw that they had been abandoned by those who had trained them and that the thirteen others who were to join them with a greater stock of munitions ten days later did not appear over the water's surface or at the edge of the white sand where they had been expected; and still again present when the winds blowing strongly over the ocean saw him disappear toward the mountains to hide with his companions—one black man and twelve pale-skin mulattoes in a country of black people.

And at last, he must have recognized the now-familiar sound when he faced death in the mountains of L'Asile with the remainder of his companions, survivors of this retreat that was a two-and-a-half-month fight against government forces—finding himself discovered and finally out of munitions, he cried, "If we must die, let us die like brave men!" And, lacking bullets, he started throwing stones.

It is bullets, then, that killed him, not decapitation.

I have waited numerous years to learn that, years spent uselessly holding up under this weight lodged in the heart of memory, personal memory and family memory.

Years to suffer this image, the emotion, the anxiety over this other death by decapitation that we always thought had been his own because of the gruesome newspaper front page photograph of his severed head that had publicized his capture.

But he is no less of a martyr, and is a political martyr for sure. But for me, and of greater importance still, he is a martyr of the faith, of *his* faith. I long thought of the day when I would stand on the beach at Dame Marie, holding a candle—humble luminary to celebrate the man with a great heart.

If it is true that one can weep eternally for a life that seems wasted, cut off too young at twenty-three, it is also true that there are hearts whose sensitivity is so great, so vibrant, so intensely impregnated by all of life's experiences, that their life is in fact, in its substance, infinitely richer, denser, more profound and, in a way, longer because it is fuller. I think of the internal journey that it must have been for Gustave, this last travel going from New York to L'Asile, stopping through Dame Marie. I see it as a rite of passage going toward what parcel of divinity he carried in him, a rite that would allow his giving birth to the Jesus of his being.

To come to Dame Marie by the road, leaving from Jeremie, means that one arrives from high up, over the hills. The church nests in the village under a vast, clear sky and shines like a pearl, first from afar and minute, then growing more and more at every turn of the road, down to the public square's small green garden, on the coastal strip, at the edge of the blue sea.

So, I was finally standing on the white sands of the beach at Dame Marie. Under the midday sun, I held a votive candle for Our Lady of Perpetual Help. It would have burnt seven days if winds allowed it—because winds always blow there, the same winds that would have pushed them, these thirteen companions, whipped them, caressed them, drunkened them, even.

I dug a small hole at the foot of a coconut tree so the candle would be stable and protected from the winds. I wedged it with sea rocks. I prayed with both the humility and presumption of prayer that requests and hopes for the well-being of the soul of the one we cherish and miss or for continued strength on its journey. But I mostly thanked Gustave for this great gift that he has made to us, his family.

More than of his life, he has made us the gift of his death. He taught us what death can offer life. Since Gustave, we carry in us this grand gesture he made of his death.

I don't think that either Uncle Edward or anyone else could have convinced him not to embark for his country. A man of great heart is forcibly a man of great dreams. Logic can do nothing against such men. A decision like the one he made does not come from the domain of reason: it comes from the most profound region of who he, Gustave, was; it is born out of a temperament that drags along with him the sensitive image of all that he has lived before he could arrive at that point, at that decision, and that pushed him to make it.

It would not have been possible to tell him, "You can neither avenge your father's death nor bring him back. Think of him who would not have wanted you to take such a risk. Think of your mother, think of yourself. This makes no sense—a handful of men cannot fight, and win, against a state."

To reason with him would not have been possible because what he was about to do was more profound than reason, more vast than vengeance, greater than himself: the call from the father was that of his soul. He found a unique moment in time that allowed him to act to the measure of his soul. Like all of us, he came on earth to surpass himself. Like very few of us, the élan in him was so strong that there was no need for a long life of dull repetitions, of meager satisfactions, vain and selfish, of reductive fears erected in the name of common sense, to finally be able to arrive, crawling and out of breath, at the foot of the Almighty.

It was standing up that Gustave presented himself to the Light.

Because he had a hero's soul.

In his *Imitation of Christ*, Thomas à Kempis wrote: "You are wrong, you are wrong if you seek anything than to suffer trials; for this whole mortal life is full of miseries and is marked on every side with crosses. The further a man advances in Spirit, so much heavier are the crosses he often finds, because the pain of his exile increases with his love. . . . Great fruit and benefit will be his by the bearing of his own cross. For while he willingly submits himself to such trial, then all the burden of tribulation is turned into assurance of divine consolation. . . . It is not the virtue of man, but the grace of God that enables a frail man to attempt and love that which by nature he abhors and fears."[1]

Hard to say how, in his childhood, Gustave knew where to glean examples and life experience that could fill and give shape to a soul with heroic appetite. Grandfather Jules acted as his father, and ours too in a way. I always had the feeling that my own father spent his life trying to live up to the bravery Grandfather showed during the First World War. For my father, no human qualities equaled the courage, loyalty, and righteousness exemplified in the character and lives of great soldiers. There is no doubt in my mind that, for Gustave the child, his grandfather, decorated with the Iron Cross, his father the colonel, and his uncles, even, were at some point *the* great men, the braves, the example to follow, the way.

One could also say that his grandmother, an ardent Christian, shaped his childhood. It is in his bedroom that she painted the life-size Saint Jude Thaddeus, patron of desperate causes, whose feet and hands I complained were too small while I watched her paint, thus making her laugh without feeling any compulsion to enlarge them. Her laughter cascaded in the air and fell like big water bodies that have unfathomable, unseen repercussions into the rock and deep in the earth; it slid down in waves along her great breasts, softened by age, until it finally went and lost itself in the large cove of her hips and belly, sitting as she was, her small legs opened up, spread out, the flowery blue cloth of her skirt pulled across the chair as is done by legs of old women who have become too fat and indifferent to their physical grace.

Gustave's laughter, on the other hand, as soon as it was carried out of his throat, which appeared to me then an unshakable column singularly marked at the disturbing point of his Adam's apple, seemed to be engulfed back down the same throat, descend all the way down his body to his feet, and die down at the earth wherefrom I would receive it, a small child, him so tall, teasing him about trivial things so he would laugh again—a child's stratagem that reveals the love felt and hides its embarrassment.

Gustave's bedroom was at the end of the hallway, straight down from the top of the stairs that I would sometimes silently crawl up to, like the Indian I imagined myself to be, in order to spy on our grandmother: she seemed large and anchored while she painted this emaciated Saint Jude whose eyes looked like two black embers in a bearded face. But actually, we were the ones who were being observed, by the gaze emanating from Gustave's portrait: a photograph hung over the little bed of all of Gustave's coddled childhood, showing Gustave in a U.S. Army uniform, a man now, standing, his right hand resting on the airplane he flew, but his head and eyes looking toward us.

Grandmother gave away her Saint Jude to the Christ-Roi Church in Bourdon where we grew up. I imagine that someone hurried to put this painting in the oubliette, in a depot, because no one knew of its existence when I inquired about it a few skinny years later.

───────

Now it is the example of Gustave-the-man that stands before us, before me. His gesture changed us and continues to transform and defy us while it lives within us. Without Gustave, we would have been different: we are who we are because Gustave was.

In his essay "Religion and Poetry," Paul Claudel wrote: "Religion did not just fill life with drama but it created at the end of it, with Death, the highest form of drama which, for any true disciple of our Divine Master, is found in sacrifice."[2] This, Gustave died to teach us. We would not do him justice and we would even be robbing ourselves of a precious gift we were bequeathed if we were not able to recognize this, admire him for it, and if we were afraid to remain as willing witnesses of a life that expressed its greatest dimension.

The town of Jeremie also remembers my cousin and godfather, and it is a face in mourning that it still bears today. Is it possible that it carries in its memory a living remorse that gnaws at and grinds its old walls, and covers them with the gray mood of a coat made from dust and refuse?

However dilapidated it has become, Jeremie still keeps its beautiful cemetery that glows on the hillside like a miniature Rome with its domes, arches, and porticos. The poet Émile Roumer is buried there.

One hears that men from Jeremie have pretensions to a kind of inspired singularity: they often succeed at it. It is one of those who, in the evening, at an Auberge Inn table, told me what he knew of Gustave's death, and this man, himself looking like a great grasshopper of a man wearing full clothes, and seen to fold his long, dry limbs over a din-maker of a motorcycle which he hangs onto like some insects do onto their wings; his high legs seem to want to make him trip over himself while he comes towards you; his hair is a fleece full of obstinate curls, white hills that start from the top of his forehead and follow one another all the way and out of sight around the curvy horizon of his head; of an eagle, he has the fixed stare: one eye that absorbs you because the man has passion, because he watches, and one eye that is no longer one but that continues to see the last image received, this eye said to have been lost at guerilla warfare of another people than ours.

He also told me about Roland's death, Gustave's father—pushed out of a plane above Jeremie's ocean. I learnt about the entire Villedonne family's death—men, women, children, and the elderly, all of them gathered naked on the airport landing strip and machine-gunned. He showed me the Villedonnes' family house and talked about his childhood friends—the Sansonne, the Chavigny, the Drouet, and many more—because Gustave was not the only one whose family came from Jeremie.

In this Haitian country, history is passed orally from one generation to the next, whether it is religious history, familial, or political. At Dame Marie, an eighteen-year-old fisherman showed me the beach where the group of *guerilleros* had landed. He understood, having only overheard me pronouncing Gustave Villedonne's name, to which exact spot he needed to take me.

The sea appears to cover all, drag all to engulf all, and forget all. On a night of a full moon at a Grande Anse beach, winds push the waves until they come and topple over each other on the beach. The same sea that delivered Gustave to the shores of Dame Marie continues to edge this island as it did our lives.

Our lives go up high like waves for only a brief moment, and then die down on the littoral. But they don't get wasted and lost there as we think—the sea takes them back, ebbs, and contains them. In its water's depth, the sea keeps the world's memory. This immensity where one would like to be dissolved, that attracts and frightens us, also allows us to touch God with the mind. Mystics say that what is below reflects what is above. In Haiti, popular belief has it that the world under the sea reflects all that is on earth. The journey underwater is a mystical voyage wherefrom one returns transformed and powerful. Sky, earth, and sea: maybe all that is but a single great canvas on which color zones touch each other without interrupting the thread. I do not know in which color zone Gustave now happens to live, but I know that he is nevertheless able to reach, and continues to touch my being in the zone where I find myself captive.

NOTES

1. à Kempis, Thomas. *Imitation of Christ*. Book 2, chapter 12, no. 7–8.
2. Claudel, Paul. "Religion et Poésie." In *Réflections sur la Poésie*. Folio Essais. Éditions Gallimard, 1963.

At the
Gate

There is a day I'll never forget: November first, it was. I had started toward Camp Roussel early—the sun would get high overhead really fast and there were no shade trees, save for a few scrawny *bayawonn*. Their small leaves were always so parched and suffocated with dust that they seemed to require your intervention and shade more than you did theirs. Even back then, women called me a skinny old man. Nevertheless, I took that dirt road with gusto every morning and watched the hills on the horizon as I walked. These hilltops of Morne à Cabrits were nothing but dry, thorny, and bareback. Goats' Mountain, the range is called, and it deserves that name. However, in my eyes, the highlands were beautiful in the distance, stretching as they did on either side of La Vigie, the only volcano in Haiti.

That November first, as usual, I turned the street corner at Pon Bedèt Insane Asylum, following its very long and high enclosing wall toward the front gate.

The street where Pon Bedèt's iron gate is located, at the end of the wall, was always busy and festive with women vendors who sat behind pyramids of fruits and vegetables. These women were forever spoiling me with free samples from their stalls. Guavas were my favorites. Had I told them that, I would have had one saved for me every single day when they were in season. But I did not want to abuse their generosity—these were poor, struggling women. It was not pride because I am a man and, as such, I am expected to have money to pay for my own needs instead of taking from women.

There is no shame in being poor. As it is, I was born poor. I was still poorer than any of them and they knew it.

None of these women had men to help out with the children. And yet, there was an endless stream of children popping out every year and never a man in sight to claim them. If I did not know better, I'd call it a miracle, each time a child was born. No wonder people keep saying "It's God that gives children." Maybe I reminded the women of some father or grandfather they once had or wished they had—they were always happy when I showed up.

"Papa Pyè! Come over here," they called as soon as they caught sight of me. "Come and chat with us!" They stretched their broadest smiles. Teeth always look so much more luminous when showing next to a woman's brilliant black skin! Ah! I remember them well!

"Good morning, ladies!" I said, lifting my hat to them. "How are you on this fine morning? How is business?"

They cheered every time I lifted my old straw hat. The peacock feather on it trembled slightly. And if ever I also was inspired to bow to them as well as lift the hat, boy! They clapped noisily.

"Today is the day you're finally gonna tell us where you live, Papa Pyè, isn't it?" one woman would say to me every morning with a playful pout.

"God willing," I'd reply, showing her a great smile of my own.

They all giggled when they'd hear me use that old popular saying, always good for the most evasive answer you need.

"What's that village where you go back every afternoon?" she'd insist, challenging me while I pretended not to hear her and to be paying attention to the others. "Tell us who takes care of this cotton jacket of yours. Come on, Papa Pyè! Tell us. That sand color on your jacket is always spotless. Come on! Who is she?"

I chatted with each and every one of them. The bits and pieces of lives are always so meaningful. And when I finally resumed my walk and continued on, I still heard calling from behind my back. "That woman sure loves you Papa Pyè! Come on, Papa Pyè! Tell us! Who is she?"

How I miss them! How I wish I could see them again! But, concerning each one of us, Life has its own mind made up from the start.

Look at me—my father scolded me all through my school years, "Go study! Do your homework!" He'd slap my ears each time I wanted to go and play. It seems that doing schoolwork or helping my mother were the only two things I was allowed to do at home up until I was sent to boarding school when I was eleven. My mother cried. My father was relieved. He kept warning me, instructing me, reminding me that education paves a man's road to wealth.

It did not turn out that way—look at me still.

If my father ever learnt that the definition of true wealth might vary, I'll never know. May his soul rest in peace! I don't know where he got these notions on the purpose and power of education. He never had any education and no more money than I ever had myself. If it weren't for charity and scholarships from the brothers of Saint Martial College in Port-au-Prince, I would have swept dirt off a dirt floor all of my life, like my father did and his father before him. And still, I never had more than a dirt floor to settle my bed over when I was a grown man, no matter how much education I ended up having.

I am and never was anything else than a poor man.

I never knew how to turn knowledge into money. And at times when I had a job, there were always so many without job and money, I ended up giving it away as fast as I earned it.

I can't help it—the poor keep coming, they keep coming at you until you are one of them, crazy from lacking everything you shouldn't be and you don't know how it got to be that way. Seeing that, no woman would stay with me.

I guess I saw I had grown up alright without any money. I saw my parents lived what I thought was a full life, and without any money. I felt I did not need to be any different from who they were. God only knows, I had the best education ever afforded any man on earth.

But, in the end, the only difference between my father and me is that education took my mind to places where my father's never traveled.

My father only imagined the wealth that money can buy whereas I received the wealth that money can't buy. I am the living proof that his dream took form and that dreams can take real form.

My own dream was that dreams should spread like bushfire until the whole land is burning. Like it is now—look around.

———————

As I was saying, it was November first, All Souls' Day.

I had again walked the distant road coming toward Miragoane. That whole region was already arid and devastated by the deforestation that has now devoured so much of Haiti. People keep cutting down trees for coal but you can't blame them—what other fuel do they have?

At any rate, that day, the vendors were nowhere to be seen except for one little girl. She sat in front of a wooden tray that contained all but Chiclets gum and a high pile of roasted peanuts.

"Ti Kal?" I asked. "Not going to school?"

"My aunt went to church. I have to stay here until she comes back."

"Is your aunt the one who found time to tie these pink bows in each of your two braids?" I asked her with a smile.

"Yes. She is, Papa Pyè," Ti Kal said, hiding her giggles with one hand over her mouth and turning her face to the side.

"She did well—you look mighty pretty, Ti Kal. I hope you sell all your peanuts soon and you can come to school. I'll be expecting you."

"Yes, Papa Pyè. Thank you, yes."

I continued on my way along the sidewalk stretching by Pon Bedèt's high wall, in the direction toward Lamorinière. That area used to be the wealthiest of plains during colonial times, and Lamorinière was one of several sugar plantations.

Anyway, as I was saying, I walked along the asylum's wall, a whitewashed cement wall that was lined from the inside with lemon trees and with violet bougainvillea whose blossoms overflowed at the top and all along the wall.

On the street side of the wall, black goats were tied to *belles mexicaines* wild vines that carpeted the dirt canal dug between the wall and the sidewalk. I tell you, the vines were blooming with an abundance of pink buds that were really wondrous to see.

My walking stopped once I reached the tall bayawonn tree that stood almost right at Pon Bedèt's green iron gate.

The gate was a simple one.

It had two panels and opened in the middle. It was made of wrought iron bars set vertically from each other at four-inch intervals. The vertical bars were held together by larger bars that were soldered horizontally, one at the base, one in the middle, and the last at the top.

Built in this way, the gate allowed patients to look out into the street and for people in the street to interact with patients. The gate therefore felt open in spite of the chain and big padlock that kept it securely shut at all times.

Pon Bedèt Insane Asylum is basically a two-acre square piece of land enclosed by a high wall.

Rooms for the patients are disposed all along three sides of the wall and leave the center free to be used as a kind of inner courtyard. Being very small, and shabbily built with only a door and no window, the rooms seem hardly more than horse stables that someone painted green and white too many years ago.

A few mango trees and coconut trees grow in the open center space, as well as one breadfruit tree, one *tchatcha* tree, and one *flamboyant* tree. The grounds are covered with sunburnt grass and weeds.

The fourth side of the square is the side along which bathrooms, the clinic, and offices were built. The gate stood in a corner of that fourth side.

On the street side of Pon Bedèt's gate, under the bayawonn tree growing there, children of various ages were waiting for me. They sat on stools or straw chairs loosely arranged around a rickety table.

Some days, there were not enough chairs to go around and some of the children had to stand. They bore their discomfort with a grace and patience not unusual in children not accustomed to living with means and ease. These were children used to rough circumstances, raised by adults with little time to spare for indulging moods and whims.

The children always greeted me joyfully. Their welcome cheered me no matter how I felt on any particular day—you know how it is for all of us on this earth; there are some days when the heart feels better than others and for no special reason.

The tree and its shade were what I called "my school." The children were "my students," all ten or twelve of them.

The number of children varied each day. They came as they could or would.

Once I had arrived, I patted a couple of heads, stroked a couple of cheeks, settled myself on a chair among them, and announced, "School's open!"

That day, November first, I had barely finished saying, "School's open!" when I overheard behind my back, "Good morning, Papa Pyè! How are you today?"

"Who is asking?" I said, turning around.

"It's me, Gadyen! Up on the wall."

"Oh, Gadyen! Funny I didn't recognize your voice."

Gadyen was a nice young man I befriended right from the time he started working at Pon Bedèt, where he was employed to watch over the patients. He had an easy manner with everyone and so he was well liked, whether by the patients or the various people related to them who would, at times, come to visit. The doctors and the staff in the small clinic liked him too, even if they had little actual contact with him.

Gadyen was most comfortable with the people he was to watch over—the insane at the asylum. He pretty much stayed around them only and that suited everyone. After all, being around the mentally ill locked up at Pon Bedèt was his job.

"I am happy to see you so early," I said. "How is your roost today?"

"My 'roost'?" Gadyen repeated after me, amused. "Papa Pyè, damn it, you're comical! My roost is fine. All of them crazy, as usual. Specially today, actually."

"Why is that?"

"I just came back from the sugar mill. It's because of Justin, the man from Port-au-Prince."

"Who?"

"Justin. The one who goes around calling out a bunch of funny names, the same ones all the time—Voltaire! Montaigne! Ronsard! He's been here since July. You've seen him."

"Oh yes . . . The mulatto. I remember. He has a sister who visits him. Right? She was talking to Altagrace the other day. You pointed it out to me because you were so surprised someone was talking to Altagrace. Is she the one?"

"Right. That's Justin's sister."

"So, what happened? Why did you have to go to the mill?"

"They found Justin on top of a pile of sugarcane on their way to the grinding machine. He was smoking a cigarette and calling out more names. It's the names that saved him actually—the machinist heard that idiot's voice and stopped the machines on 'Descartes!' in the nick of time. If it weren't for that, Justin'd be history-and-pulp by now."

"Thank God for French philosophers," I said.

"French who?"

"Writers—the names Justin is calling out all day. But tell me, do Altagrace and Justin's sister know each other from before Pon Bedèt?"

"I wouldn't know," Gadyen said. "And how is *your* roost today?"

"I just arrived but the children seem fine. Except for Ti Kal— she is selling peanuts for her aunt this morning."

"What is she going to miss out on anyway, Papa Pyè?" Gadyen said with that sideways smirk he sometimes chose to tease me. "They are just counting rubber bands, aren't they?"

"Yes, they are," I replied, lifting my chin up with arrogance he would have known was only play. "Rubber bands are what I have to offer. And, we're going to cross to the new millennium counting rubber bands, and while doing that, not only will we know *how* to count but we will also realize that *we* count as well." I took my hat off, hung it on the back of my chair and turned my back on Gadyen.

"Gadyen, you know what a millennium is?" I asked while my back was still turned.

"I know what a millennium is."

Gadyen's tone made me curious. I turned around in time to see him take his red cap off, put his hand to his heart, and look up to the sky.

"Of course, I know what a millennium is," he said again. "God himself explained it all to me."

"Good," I said. "That settles it then."

"Yes it does."

"My father used to tell me the world belongs to those who rise early," I said, "but I believe the world belongs to those who can count." While I spoke, I emptied my pants pockets of a huge amount of rubber bands. I spread them loosely on the table and the children grabbed at them right away.

"Even *rubber bands*? Even count *rubber bands*?" Gadyen asked.

"Yes, rubber bands. Or anything else you wish to."

"That does 'settles' it then," he said.

"Good. But, tell me, where is your guardian angel, this Jistinvil who can't seem to be able to let you out of his sight?"

"Jistinvil is in bed."

"What for?"

"Protesting."

"What for?"

"Jistinvil is protesting that today is All Souls' Day and he wants to go to Saint Yves's."

"What for?"

"He loves pilgrimages," Gadyen said with a smile, and then, with a lowered voice, "Jistinvil also has warned us that Saint Yves will bring a curse to this place if we don't let people go to his shrine when they want to."

"There is something to be said for pilgrimages," I said, "although today is not Saint Yves's day or even All Saints' Day, it's All *Souls'* Day. But, I agree with Jistinvil, one should go and pay respect to the Saints—they are great teachers."

"From the look of Jistinvil, today *is* All Souls' Day alright," Gadyen said, "because Jistinvil looks like Death itself." At that, Gadyen stretched himself stiffly on top of the wall to imitate Jistinvil in bed.

"The Dead are great teachers," I said.

"Great teachers of what?" Gadyen asked with a mocking tone while sitting back up. "And speaking of teachers, why not have the kids count thorns on the tree you sit under every single day that God makes instead of counting rubber bands?"

"Aha! A good science project you are suggesting here! But, how do we get up the tree?" I asked.

"I've got just the thing!" Gadyen cried with great excitement. "Pon Bedèt's ladder!"

At that, Gadyen jumped off the wall so fast that he knocked down one of the patients standing at the gate watching passersby.

"No!" I said quickly. "No ladder."

Gadyen stopped short.

"Why not?" he asked, looking disappointed and perplexed.

"Ladders are not a good thing," I said.

"Why is that? What's wrong with ladders?" Gadyen now looked visibly annoyed.

"It's obvious," I said flatly.

But patients at the gate had overheard us and they felt about the ladder the way Gadyen did.

"LA-DDER! LA-DDER!" The patients started to shout together in unison, repeatedly and enthusiastically like an anthem.

Gadyen was grinning furiously and opened his arms wide as if to tell me, "You see, old fool, even the nuts in here have more sense than you do and know a good idea when they hear one."

But I was never one to be intimidated by group pressure. "Maybe the crazies in there should be watching you instead of you watching them," I said.

But just then, I heard noises from what sounded like a brawl happening in the common courtyard. This called for Gadyen's attention as well, and off he went inside in a hurry saying with a grin, "Don't think I am done with you, old man."

Under the bayawonn tree outside, I then turned my attention to the children. I took a stick out of my jacket and tapped three times on the table. This was the usual way I started class. The children liked this little ritual.

"Riben!" I called to a willowy boy on my right. "*You* start counting."

He was new to the school and had an eagerness I loved. I remember how proud he looked when he did well and I congratulated him. This child had natural self-respect. He had a sense of the honor I did him when I started school, choosing him to be the first one to count.

I did not notice that Gadyen was already back on top of the wall.

"Papa Pyè!" Gadyen called, startling me. "You were kind of right—maybe the crazies in there should be watching me instead of me watching them."

"How's that?" I asked suspiciously, turning around to face him.

"I grew up being watched by who I was watching—that's the way of my life."

"How's that?"

"I grew up with my grandmother," he said.

"Why is that?"

"The usual story . . . but never mind that," he said. "Thatch-and-mud house. One room, it was. She slept on a mat outside—she liked stars. She said she would soon enough be closed up in a box when she was dead, she didn't need to do it when she was alive." Gadyen crossed his arms over while he studied my face. "She watched after me—I was just a boy. I watched after her—she was a brittle old thing. And the chicken watched out for both of us." He laughed.

"Did you go to school?"

"My grandmother's tongue was my school," he said abruptly. "And that thing never gave me recess. Could be wicked too. But she liked me. Anyway, she had to—I was all she had. She was all I had."

"Listening is a good way of learning," I said.

"Not when it's your grandmother and she won't shut up!" Gadyen laughed.

"In my school, however, there are all kinds of teachers, not just me—the students learn from observation as well. In my school, *you're* a teacher too."

"How's that?" Gadyen looked amused but seemed to scrutinize me to find out if I was making fun of him. "What do I teach?"

"Human Resources."

"What's that?"

"Listen," I said, "why do you think I settled my school right in front of Pon Bedèt's gate a few months ago? And, it so happens, it was just a few days before you came to work here."

"And why did you settle here?"

"I have been studying them—the patients, I mean— and that whole situation at the asylum. I think the time is ripe; they are ready—from now on, all your crazies will be teachers too. I saw that Pon Bedèt was a blessed gift to me, a specialized school waiting to be discovered and opened up."

"You're putting me on?" Gadyen's lower lip hung down as if in stupor while his eyebrows rose up high in astonishment.

"No Gadyen, I am not putting you on." I was firm about that.

"Yeah? And so, what will the crazies teach?" he asked, raising his chin at me defiantly.

"Clinical Psychology. That's what."

"Clinical what? What the *hell* are you talking about Papa Pyè?" Gadyen was upset. "I never knew you to be a mean old man. I had already figured you out for a nut no better than the ones in here. I saw that. But mean, I did not see that—talking above a man's head and making fun of a man because he did not go to school and there are some words he doesn't know? No. That's not right." Gadyen turned his red cap backward and I noticed the gesture—it was always a sign that something in him was disquieted and, literally, turned around. I had seen him do that before when I watched him dealing with patients and things had gotten out of hand.

"No Gadyen," I said reassuringly. "I never mean to make fun of anyone. I am dead serious. Things will become clear very soon. I will explain. Just give me a little time, and listen."

"I've done plenty of listening," he said with a pout.

"Come on, help me out," I said. "I am only sharing my ideas

with you. And do you know what more I have been thinking about?"

"What's that?" Gadyen could always be counted on to be curious.

"Ti Kal's aunt who sits under this hot Caribbean sun all day long whispering 'Jesus, Mary, Joseph' every time someone looks at her goods, who lights a candle under her stall at the risk of setting it on fire, who sprinkles corn kernels under her feet for the Spirits while she wants you to think it is for stray chicken, who drops everything to go to mass on All Souls' Day, who counts her money at the end of the day and decides how much of it she can spend to feed Ti Kal and the whole pack of her own children, and who figures out how much to reinvest in more Chiclets and peanuts—well, Gadyen, Ti Kal's aunt, she too will be a teacher in my school."

"Oh yeah?" Gadyen said with a sneer. "And just what will she teach?"

"Philosophy of Religion *and* Business Administration," I said flatly, all in one breath, sure to impress him now. "I have now found the solution to all my problems, figured out the theorem of a lifetime of investigation, the equation of heavenly aesthetics. I have creatively overcome my economic difficulties and found new ways of establishing and maintaining a meaningful modern school for the children of Haiti, a school that faces outright the existing limitations of the environment and responds to the unique situation in which this country finds itself while it continues to struggle courageously."

Gadyen now looked totally irritated. I was disconcerted by the expression on his face and was about to explain myself further when he jumped off the wall into the street side of Pon Bedèt's gate and walked head on toward me.

There was an instant uproar from the patients who stood and crowded at the gate, complaining they would not be able to overhear Gadyen and me—they wanted to follow our conversation.

Gadyen turned around and, facing them, took out a police whistle from his shirt pocket. They instantly quieted down even before he had to blow the whistle. He turned back to me.

"Hear this, Papa Pyè," he said coldly and disdainfully. "That tree will get mad at you some day. And hear this again, you stand under its shade and make that shade your classroom as if you owned tree, shade, and sidewalk."

I was speechless.

Gadyen continued, "I warn you: have the kids count those thorns and acknowledge the tree as your science teacher like I told you earlier when I said I wasn't finished with you about the ladder and counting those thorns on the tree, remember? Show the tree respect—light a candle to it, pour a little rum. Without that tree, you don't have a school. No place to stand. You'd be just a poor old man in the street. You're spreading big words and you think you're a big-time philosopher when you're just big-time crazy." Gadyen eyed me down for a few seconds as if he dared me to respond. "Besides, I need to know how many thorns live on this tree." At that he smiled mysteriously and turned his heels on me.

"Why is that?" I asked, following him.

"I need a number for the lottery. Altagrace gave me a dollar bill."

"That's a perfectly good reason," I said. "And how is Altagrace?"

"The same." Gadyen faced the asylum and pointed to a spot a few feet away from the gate, inside the courtyard. "The same," he repeated with a low voice. "Sitting there all day and every day."

"What did she say when she gave you the dollar bill?"

"Altagrace never speaks."

"I wonder, how long is it since she's been in there by now?"

"I don't know. I don't keep track of those things. That's not my job, Papa Pyè. She just gave me a dollar bill. That's all I know."

"La Veyèz, for sure, would know," I said. "Is it true that . . ."

"HOLD IT! WHO IS SAYING MY NAME?" We heard ourselves addressed by a very loud, cheerful voice calling from behind. "WHO FEELS FREE TO MENTION ME WHEN I AM NOT THERE?"

"La Veyèz!" Gadyen exclaimed with pleasure.

I turned around to find La Veyèz laughing and standing near the children, fists propped on her hips. She was dressed all in black, including purse, shoes, stockings, hat, and sunglasses. She had come on the bus that brought the cooks who made food for the asylum's patients, all two hundred of them, give or take.

Coming out of the bus amidst the cooks who wore all manner

of colorful designs on their dresses, La Veyèz looked like an eggplant emerging out of a fruit basket.

The cooks unloaded their pots and pans from the bus's rooftop. Their behinds looked as wide and round as their baskets. The patients gathered at the gate like a pack of agitated crows to watch the cooks settle themselves on the sidewalk, just a few feet away from "my" bayawonn tree school.

"But today is not Friday, is it?" I asked La Veyèz.

"Nope. Today is not Friday, the day I come here to watch that she-demon Altagrace." She pursed her lower lip out in a show of disgust at the mere mention of the name. "This may be Haiti where we're treated like animals, but today is All Souls' Day and, somehow, I got the day off."

She stopped and walked closer to me with her index finger pointing at me from the bridge of her flat nose, nostrils arched like a bull's. She was not a pretty woman. She was fat. She was wonderfully alive.

"I came straight from church," she said, "to watch *her* that sits in there as if she's human. I want to make sure she never, ever, comes out of Pon Bedèt and back in my neighborhood." La Veyèz took a deep breath and spoke again with a threatening tone. "She's lucky she's locked up!" She then agitated her gloved hands like black puppets to help her state a final point: "I wish she'd come out. I would gladly choke her dead with these."

"What kind of Christian talk is that?" I said, feeling stunned by how brazen she was, but somewhat amused also—we all knew what brought La Veyèz to Pon Bedèt every Friday.

"Some deaths God agrees with. Some he does not," La Veyèz said, pointing a stiff, black finger to the sky. "I'll tell you a story. Listen to me: I had surgery; everything went fine. But one day, my stitches come undone—blood all over. I pass out. People I don't even know take me to the hospital. Doctors say I am dead. In my mind I came to a dark country. Not a bit of light." At that, La Veyèz lowered her face to the children and said with a mysterious tone, "'Have I come to the place of the dark unknown? Am I dead?' I asked." Then, La Veyèz got quiet, straightened herself, and looked at me right in the eyes, speaking with foreboding. "When there's darkness, it's not sent by God. That's why I was brought back to this world—I have a message."

"How did you get out of that 'daaark country'?" Gadyen asked. He could never resist teasing La Veyèz. It was an easy and tempting job, I must admit.

"You can laugh, Gadyen," she said contemptuously, unaffected by his mockery. "The fact is: He wanted me to serve Him in this world so He resuscitated me." La Veyèz backed up and stood in the middle of the street, under the sun, in full view and earshot of all who walked by. "Once I was cured, I converted." She spoke with conviction. "I won't serve Spirits. I got GOD with me!"

La Veyèz looked around her. People in the street showed no interest in her and were going about their business. She then walked closer to the gate and to the eager audience of patients. They waved their arms and hands in between the gate's bars to invite her closer still.

Gadyen quickly went past her, unlocked the gate to let himself in, slipped back inside, locked the gate again and stood guard there while I turned my attention back to the children. The school day had been very interrupted until then.

"Jilyen! Ti Fi! Zoban! Kids!" I called. "Who's counting? Ah, it's Zoban? OK Zoban. Start counting." The boy's voice rose with hesitation.

"First rubber band . . . second rubber band . . . third rubber band . . ."

"Very gooood . . . go on Zoban," I encouraged him.

". . . seventh rubber band . . . eighth rubber band . . ."

I then turned around again and said to Gadyen at the gate, "You saw *in action* what I was telling you earlier."

"What's that?" he asked, mildly interested.

"La Veyèz as Anthropology of Religion teacher!"

La Veyèz turned about-face. "What's Papa Pyè talking about?"

"I want to understand something about you, La Veyèz," I said with a maliciously teasing tone. "What's this All Souls' Day reverence of yours about if you don't serve 'Spirits'? After all, the Dead are Spirits, aren't they? You just went to a church *ceremony* for them, didn't you?"

"STOP!" Gadyen suddenly yelled. He opened the gate again and rushed out swiftly. "Papa Pyè, All Souls' Day is no joke," he said sternly and fearfully.

"It was just a question," I said, pretending innocence.

"I know about your questions," he said. He then pulled La Veyèz and me away from the children and the patients. The children started whispering excitedly with hands cupped to each other's ears and the patients started hooting for all in the neighborhood to overhear. Gadyen pulled out his whistle—the hooting stopped. Then, he said to us in a hushed voice, "Spirits can hear you, the Dead can see you: respect them! They are shadows that live where there is quiet."

"Oh yes?" I said. "Drums beating all night long during ceremonies for Spirits, *that's* quiet?"

"Music is an invitation," Gadyen explained thoughtfully. "Spirits respond to it. Earth Spirits come like wind, Fire Spirits like lightning, Water Spirits like reflections, and . . ."

"That's it!" I exclaimed with great excitement. "A poet! Poetry workshop! Gadyen! That's the real job for you! I have discovered who you really are!"

Gadyen ignored me totally, contemptuous. He continued on his own tracks about Spirits, saying, "La Veyèz can brag about God who loves *her* since she converted and . . ."

"Watch your mouth!" La Veyèz snapped.

". . . she can complain about Altagrace," Gadyen continued, "and accuse her of loving blood . . ."

"SHE DOES LOVE BLOOD!"

". . . like she has been telling us every Friday till we can't listen to it anymore, but Spirits? They are real. Werewolves, they are real."

"Spirits are one thing, Gadyen," I interrupted him, "and werewolves are another. You mix everything up."

"What do you know about Spirits anyway? I thought you only respect *science*?" La Veyèz snapped at me.

"La Veyèz," Gadyen intervened, "don't bug Papa Pyè."

"What's it to you if I do, crazies-nanny?" she barked at him.

"Let me tell you about werewolves," Gadyen said, undisturbed by La Veyèz's insult or by my previous criticism. "They can take any shape. Let me tell you: one time, it's the middle of the night. Suddenly, I wake up. Just then, a cat crosses over me! I grab the stick by my pillow and hit the cat. It runs to the door. I run after it and hit, and hit, and hit . . . but the cat runs away anyway . . ."

"A hungry cat," I said.

"Oh yeah?" Gadyen sneered. "Well, let me tell you that, next morning, half the people in the neighborhood say 'Good morning' to me, the other half don't. Little old man sitting on a little straw chair, I tell him, 'Good morning!' He gives me the finger. Next morning I tell him, 'Good morning!' He gives me the finger. I walk away but watch him from the corner of my eye. I see him trying to get up but it's like he doesn't have one straight bone left in his body—he can't get up. I think, OK Chief, what you deserve is what you got. Believe me or not, third day, Little Old Man was dead."

"I guess you and I are better off counting thorns in the daytime than cats at night," I told Gadyen, trying hard to hold my laughter, "because science and I have never set eyes on any werewolf."

"Yes you have!" La Veyèz interjected. "Altagrace! How about Altagrace—she is a werewolf! But I ain't afraid of her or any werewolf." La Veyèz bent forward as if she wanted to tell us a secret and spoke in a tone she hoped would sound mysterious. "One night, I saw a demon standing with many heads, each one lit up like a furnace. I ignored the demon. He flew away."

"Gadyen?" I asked. "Do you think that if Altagrace ignored her, La Veyèz would fly away too?"

"Calling me a demon!?" La Veyèz yelled. "I'll knock your head off and make you see demons like they were stars!"

"The worst demons," Gadyen said calmly, "are the Sanpwèl with their red flag. At midnight, you see their chief standing in the middle of the crossroads. He looks to the east, his arms are up and wide open—he is praying. He starts with the Hail Mary and . . ."

"SACRILEGE!" La Veyèz screamed.

"From Poetry with Gadyen," I cried ecstatically, "to Folklore with La Veyèz—believe me, I'm never moving my school out of Pon Bedèt's gate!"

". . . after that," Gadyen kept talking unperturbed, "the Sanpwèl chief salutes the west, the north, the south. When he is done, they all open their arms like wings, swing them around and around repeating, 'The crossroads are mine! The crossroads are mine!' Watch out for those: they're werewolves."

"You mean to say," I asked Gadyen, "that if La Veyèz is right and Altagrace wasn't locked up in here, she'd fly around at night singing, 'The crossroads are mine! The crossroads are mine'?"

"That's right!" La Veyèz was outraged.

"Sociology of Mythology teacher!" I cried, winking at Gadyen, but he looked away.

"Anyway, I don't need to remember that stuff," argued La Veyèz, "because I've got a *laryèt* leaf always with me."

"What's that?" I asked.

"Ha!" exclaimed Gadyen. "It's *your* turn to ask 'What's that?'" He sneered at me. "Laryèt is for protection. Everybody knows that. But, where do you keep it, La Veyèz?" Gadyen started to poke playfully into La Veyèz's ribs.

She giggled, screamed, and ran to hide behind me. Gadyen ran after her. They started running around in circles with me standing in the middle like a center post. Patients at the gate were whistling and yelling, "GET HER! GET HER!" La Veyèz kept screaming, "Stop poking me! I'll tell you, I'll tell you where I keep the laryèt," but she was not telling, until I finally caught ahold of her and held her firmly.

"It's in my wallet!" she said. "Let me go!" She was laughing.

Gadyen grinned at me with satisfaction.

"Tell me, Gadyen," I asked, "I am puzzled: into how many splinters do broken bones multiply when a small smashed cat turns back into a big old man? I mean, you do realize there are more bones in a man than in a cat, and if you want to count countless tiny thorns with me maybe we ought to practice on splinters transferred from a cat's body to a man's. What do you say?"

"If Gadyen had laryèt," La Veyèz said, interrupting me, "no demon cat would get into his house. I'll get you all some."

"No thank you," I said.

"I'll take some!" Gadyen said quickly.

The patients started hooting, "WE WILL TOO! WE WILL TOO!"

"I know some bigger demon than your demon with many heads," Gadyen whispered to La Veyèz, but loud enough for me to hear and ignoring my previous bait about the bones. "In Roseau," he said, "there's a pond they call La Rodròg that has a demon with a huge wasps' nest stuck on his face like a beard that's buzzing. People need water but nobody can get near the pond because of him."

"Wear laryèt! That'll fix him," La Veyèz said in a hushed voice and with a self-assured nod. "He'll smell it before you are even near the water. He'll stay under. You can be sure of that!"

The patients were banging on the gate all in chorus, "WE WANNA HEAR! WE WANNA HEAR!"

"Enough of this nonsense!" I said finally to Gadyen and La Veyèz with sudden exasperation. "What we need is a new Haiti with *science* blossoming in the children, not *magic.*"

"Not *science*," La Veyèz argued in a loud voice, "God!"

The patients behind the gate started jumping up and down, yelling in unison, "GOD! WE WANT GOD! WE WANT GOD!"

"God, yes," I admitted, "but, a child needs a real thing that can be seen, touched and . . ."

"Speech time!" Gadyen cried, interrupting me sarcastically, rolling his eyes. Then, he headed back toward the asylum, unlocked the gate, and walked in, wildly applauded by enthusiastic patients.

"Nothing is too small," I said, turning to La Veyèz. "Ants. Pebbles. Rubber bands. What we need is to deal with *concrete* things." La Veyèz looked at me as if I had just landed and did not understand where I was. I ignored it and said in a mock-distracted way, "but if I wanted to talk about magic and demons, I could outdo both of you."

A little spark suddenly showed in La Veyèz's eyes.

"My grandfather," I said with a confident but low voice that forced her to lean toward me so she could hear better, "could plant a breadfruit seedling in the morning and in the evening he'd pick fruits from it; the skin of sugarcane was his raft and the shell of a peanut was his canoe."

"I have heard of these things," La Veyèz said with real interest and respect, visibly hoping to hear more of my story.

"But, never mind," I said, and turned to the children, ignoring La Veyèz. "Who's doing the counting now? Who? It's Zilma? OK, Ti Zilma, show us. Start counting. I am listening."

"One rubber band . . . two rubber bands . . ." Zilma had a shy demeanor and a high-pitched voice like a bird that's straining to

sing. ". . . three rubber bands . . . twenty-three rubber bands . . .
thirty-two rubber bands . . ."

I admit that I could not focus on Zilma's counting that day, and
noticed neither her mistakes nor that Gadyen got back on top of
the wall, overhearing us. I was preoccupied.

"La Veyèz?" I asked. "What's the thing you know about Altagrace that Gadyen or I don't know? What is it about this beautiful
young woman that makes you come here every Friday, hoping to
see her dead someday soon? What happened?"

"She eats children."

"How do you know that?"

"I know: she is always alone, looking at other people's children
when we walk by."

"I don't have children either, La Veyèz. Do you think I walk on
my neighbors' roofs at night to catch some child for dinner?"

"Maybe."

"What do you mean 'maybe'?"

"Listen, Papa Pyè, I already lost three children to that she-
demon," she said. "Jean-Claude is the only one she couldn't get."

"Hey! La Veyèz! How come you don't bring Jean-Claude out
here to count rubber bands in Papa Pyè's modern-Haiti school?"
Gadyen asked from the top of the wall, startling me.

"Gadyen, let the woman talk," I snapped impatiently.

Gadyen only giggled, pleased with himself.

"I was pregnant with Jean-Claude," La Veyèz said, frowning.
"A stone hit the child in my belly. I bent down to pick up the stone
and I saw a black dog that swung quickly into Altagrace' s yard. It
was her! I know it! I took the stone home, boiled it and drank the
water. Then, I put the stone in a bucket and pissed on it. I went
out, I threw the stone back at Altagrace—now, Jean-Claude was
born healthy. Nothing can touch him." Having told her story, La
Veyèz made one of the children get up. She grabbed his chair, sat
down heavily, pulled a black handkerchief out of her black purse
and wiped the sweat from her black face. There was a silence.

"Gadyen is right. Bring your boy over next time," I said.

"Never mind that now," Gadyen interjected from above before

jumping off the wall again and down into the street. He walked toward La Veyèz, saying, "What I want to know is this: why boil the stone if you have the laryèt?"

La Veyèz sighed. "More protection is better than less."

"Listen," Gadyen said, keeping his voice low. "If your eyes don't meet the demon's eyes, he can't eat you. If you feel that a thing follows you, or hits you, don't turn around or it'll eat your soul. Just walk away . . . Pissing is just piss."

"Your mouth is yours," La Veyèz said, indignant. "Give it all the useless running you want and I'll keep pissing on stones."

"Hey, you two! Anyone ever pissed at a cat on a roof?" I asked.

"Everyday . . ." Gadyen said.

"Everyday!?"

"Everyday," Gadyen said again, casting me an indignant look, "I come in here to watch over the crazies in Pon Bedèt. Everyday, this one curses, that one cries, this one bickers with everyone, that one yells, complains, steals, lies, hides, hates everything happy. But, Altagrace—peaceful—she sleeps all night like her conscience is as clear as a butterfly's."

"Doesn't fool me!" La Veyèz said.

Gadyen ignored her. "I heard that people brought her here one night all roped up like a pig on market day and they declared she is a werewolf. They had heard a cat on a roof—meow, meow, meow—and, for them, it was Altagrace."

"IT WAS!" La Veyèz yelled with fury as if she were taking the world as witness.

"It's not just old men then that change into cat-on-the-roof?" I said with a chuckle.

Gadyen continued with his story, indifferent to any teasing or comments. "They said they heard the cat and they went to grab it just when it ran off to go and get back into *her* skin." Gadyen looked so transfixed you'd think he had been there in person and was remembering the scene. "They rushed after the cat to look for the skin in the house, try to find it before she got to it herself— they all know that werewolves have to take their skin off and hide it somewhere before they can prowl in the night. They wanted to sprinkle hot pepper on it—that way, she wouldn't be able to put it back on—it would burn, it would be hell."

"Where she belongs . . ." La Veyèz muttered in a cold voice.

Gadyen went on, "But before they could find any jar with the skin, they found Altagrace sitting quietly at home. They jumped on her anyway. A doctor lived in the neighborhood. He came out to see what was all the commotion about. He found a crowd surrounding a woman, everybody saying how they caught themselves a werewolf and they're going to kill her."

"That's right!" La Veyèz said, glaring at us. "Wish to hell we had."

But Gadyen remained unperturbed by any interruptions and kept talking as if he was having a vision and was describing it. "The doctor told them to bring her here to Pon Bedèt or he'd call the police . . ."

"That's right!"

". . . and here she is locked up forever where she makes no trouble ever. I believe in werewolves but Altagrace is not one of them. No sir. She is not."

"And you're an idiot! She makes no trouble because I make sure she *stays* locked up," La Veyèz said fiercely.

All the while Gadyen was telling Altagrace's story, the patients were shaking the gate and banging on it with stones. They felt something interesting was being discussed. They were frustrated not to be able to hear and participate.

In spite of all the noise coming from the gate, La Veyèz was still anxious to insist on her point and prove it to us.

"What you have to understand," she said, "is, here in Pon Bedèt, Altagrace can't do her demon work because everybody would notice. Only food she gets now is what's served in here and I hope to God it's bad."

"Bitch," Gadyen barked.

"Sissy!" La Veyèz hissed.

The patients were now making hissing noises too and mock-howling like dogs in distress. Gadyen got his whistle out again. They stopped.

"Talk about God all the time, but you're one mean woman," Gadyen growled, putting the whistle back in his pocket.

"Stinking hick!" La Veyèz jeered.

"Ooh . . . What kind of talk is that?" I intervened, trying to hush them. "Friends! We are friends. And there are children here."

"Stick to rubber bands, Papa Pyè! Gadyen here has got my goat and I'll get his."

"Goat is right. I got your goat because you already look like one."

"And you, you look like a macaque."

"Goat! Goat! Goat!" Gadyen trumpeted, getting into a little hopping dance.

The patients started chanting in chorus, "GOAT! GOAT! GOAT!"

La Veyèz grabbed her chair and was about to throw it at Gadyen. People walking in the street stopped to watch. They were laughing.

"Friends! What example is this for the kids? Look at the . . . Oh! GADYEN! Look! Altagrace is up on the wall! She is opening her arms! She is going to jump!"

Gadyen looked and screamed: "ALTAGRACE! STOP! WAIT!"

And then La Veyèz screamed: "CATCH THAT DEMON, GADYEN, or I'll have GOD skin you ALIVE! THIEF! Fire! FIRE! Police! POOLIIIIICE!!!!"

The patients were delirious, gleefully jumping up and down, holding hands and singing a popular children's song:

"Se ti fi a ki kwit on poul
Poul la pete chodyè,
Poul la vole l ale, pa pale!
pa paleeee!"—
"IT'S A GIRL COOKING A CHICK!
CHICKEN BREAKS DOWN THE POT!
CHICKEN FLIES AWAY GONE! HUSH IT NOW,
HUSH HUSH HUSH!"

La Veyèz started running after Altagrace, clutching her purse. I called after her: "La Veyèz! Come back! You'll never catch her! Altagrace is already too far!"

Meanwhile, Gadyen was in shock, repeating over and over, "Wow . . . Altagrace escaped . . . What am I going to say . . . What am I going to do . . ." as if he was trying to make what happened really sink in. And then he turned to me and said, "Look at Altagrace run, Papa Pyè . . . I am going to lose my job . . ."

"What a thing!" I exclaimed, baffled. "Gadyen, did you see how she opened her arms before she jumped? Kids! Did you see her too?"

For me, it was like a miracle had happened. Then, it dawned on me. "Where can she go? She is crazy . . ."

"Yeah. That's what they say she is," Gadyen said dreamily.

"Hey? Papa Pyè? You know what?"

"What?"

"I guess La Veyèz will be pissing on stones again, hey?"

"I guess she will."

Now every day I wonder how far Altagrace did make it. And today I wish I could be the one running. I wish I could see all of them once again. But I am being watched all day now. They won't let me out of their sight for one minute. They won't let me out at all. I am inside forever.